THE RED DUST

THE RED DUST

by Murray Leinster

PREY

The sky grew gray and then almost white. The overhanging banks of clouds seemed to withdraw a little from the steaming earth. Haze that hung always among the mushroom forests and above the fungus hills grew more tenuous, and the slow and misty rain that dripped the whole night long ceased reluctantly.

As far as the eye could see a mad world stretched out, a world of insensate cruelties and strange, fierce maternal solicitudes. The insects of the night—the great moths whose wings spread far and wide in the dimness, and the huge fireflies, four feet in length, whose beacons made the earth glow in their pale, weird light—the insects of the night had sought their hiding-places.

Now the creatures of the day ventured forth. A great ant-hill towered a hundred feet in the air. Upon its gravel and boulder-strewn side a commotion became visible.

The earth crumbled, and fell into an invisible opening, then a dark chasm appeared, and two slender, threadlike antennæ peered out.

A warrior ant emerged, and stood for an instant in the daylight, looking all about for signs of danger to the ant-city. He was all of ten inches long, this ant, and his mandibles were fierce and strong. A second and third warrior came from the inside of the ant-hill, and ran with tiny clickings about the hillock, waving their antennæ restlessly, searching, ever searching for a menace to their city.

They returned to the gateway from which they had made their appearance, evidently bearing reassuring messages, because shortly after they had reëntered the gateway of the ant-city, a flood of black, ill-smelling workers poured out of the opening and dispersed upon their business. The clickings of their limbs and an occasional whining stridulation made an incessant sound as they scattered over the earth, foraging among the mushrooms and giant cabbages, among the rubbish-heaps of the gigantic bee-hives and wasp colonies, and among the remains of the tragedies of the night for food for their city.

The city of the ants had begun its daily toil, toil in which every one shared without supervision or coercion. Deep in the recesses of the pyramid galleries were hollowed out and winding passages that led down a fathomless distance into the earth below.

Somewhere in the maze of tunnels there was a royal apartment, in which the queen-ant reposed, waited upon by assiduous courtiers, fed by royal stewards, and combed and rubbed by the hands of her subjects and children.

But even the huge monarch of the city had her constant and pressing duty of maternity. A dozen times the size of her largest loyal servant, she was no less bound by the unwritten but imperative laws of the city than they. From the time of waking to the time of rest, she was ordained to be the queen-mother in the strictest and most literal sense of the word, for at intervals to be measured only in terms of minutes she brought forth a single egg, perhaps three inches in length, which was instantly seized by one of her eager attendants and carried in haste to the municipal nursery.

There it was placed in a tiny cell a foot or more in length until a sac-shaped grub appeared, all soft, white body save for a tiny mouth. Then the nurses took it in charge and fed it with curious, tender gestures until it had waxed large and fat and slept the sleep of metamorphosis. When it emerged from its rudimentary cocoon it took the places of its nurses until its soft skin had hardened into the horny armor of the workers and soldiers, and then it joined the throng of workers that poured out from the city at dawn to forage for food, to bring back its finds and to share with the warriors and the nurses, the drone males and the young queens, and all the other members of its communities, their duties in the city itself. That was the life of the social insect, absolute devotion to the cause of its city, utter abnegation of self-interest for the sake of its fellows—and death at their hands when their usefulness was past. They neither knew nor expected more or less.

It is a strange instinct that prompts these creatures to devote their lives to their city, taking no smallest thought for their individual good, without even the call of maternity or sex to guide them. Only the queen knows motherhood. The others know nothing but toil, for purposes they do not understand, and to an end of which they cannot dream. At intervals all over the world of Burl's time these ant-cities rose above the surrounding ground, some small and barely begun, and others ancient colonies which were truly the continuation of cities first built when the ants were insects to be crushed beneath the feet of men. These ancient strongholds towered two, three, and even four hundred feet above the plains, and their inhabitants would have had to be numbered in millions if not billions.

Not all the earth was subject to the ants, however. Bees and wasps and more deadly creatures crawled over and flew above its surface. The bees were four feet and more in length. And slender-waisted wasps darted here and there, preying upon the colossal crickets that sang deep bass music to their mates—and the length of the crickets was the length of a man, and more.

Spiders with bloated bellies waited, motionless, in their snares, whose threads were the size of small cables, waiting for some luckless giant insect to be entangled in the gummy traps. And butterflies fluttered over the festering plains of this new world, tremendous creatures whose wings could only be measured in terms of yards.

An outcropping of rock jutted up abruptly from a fungus-covered plain. Shelf-fungi and strangely colored molds stained the stone until the shining quartz was hidden almost completely from view, but the whole glistened like tinted crystal from the dank wetness of the night. Little wisps of vapor curled away from the slopes as the moisture was taken up by the already moisture-laden air.

Seen from a distance, the outcropping of rock looked innocent and still, but a nearer view showed many things.

Here a hunting wasp had come upon a gray worm, and was methodically inserting its sting into each of the twelve segments of the faintly writhing creature. Presently the worm would be completely paralyzed, and would be carried to the burrow of the wasp, where an egg would be laid upon it, from which a tiny maggot would presently hatch. Then weeks of agony for the great gray worm, conscious, but unable to move, while the maggot fed upon its living flesh—

There the tiny spider, youngest of hatchlings, barely four inches across, stealthily stalked some other still tinier mite, the little, many-legged larva of the oil-beetle, known as the bee-louse. The almost

7

infinitely small bee-louse was barely two inches long, and could easily hide in the thick fur of a great bumblebee.

This one small creature would never fulfill its destiny, however. The hatchling spider sprang—it was a combat of midgets which was soon over. When the spider had grown and was feared as a huge, black-bellied tarantula, it would slay monster crickets with the same ease and the same implacable ferocity.

The outcropping of rock looked still and innocent. There was one point where it overhung, forming a shelf, beneath which the stone fell away in a sheer-drop. Many colored fungus growths covered the rock, making it a riot of tints and shades. But hanging from the rooflike projection of the stone there was a strange, drab-white object. It was in the shape of half a globe, perhaps six feet by six feet at its largest. A number of little semicircular doors were fixed about its sides, like inverted arches, each closed by a blank wall. One of them would open, but only one.

The house was like the half of a pallid orange, fastened to the roof of rock. Thick cables stretched in every direction for yards upon yards, anchoring the habitation firmly, but the most striking of the things about the house—still and quiet and innocent, like all the rest of the rock outcropping—were the ghastly trophies fastened to the outer walls and hanging from long silken chains below.

Here was the hind leg of one of the smaller beetles. There was the wing-case of a flying creature. Here a snail-shell, two feet in diameter, hanging at the end of an inch-thick cable. There a boulder that must have weighed thirty or forty pounds, dangling in similar fashion.

But fastened here and there, haphazard and irregularly, were other more repulsive remnants. The shrunken head-armor of a beetle, the fierce jaws of a cricket—the pitiful shreds of a hundred creatures that had formed forgotten meals for the bloated insect within the home.

Comparatively small as was the nest of the clotho spider, it was decorated as no ogre's castle had ever been adorned—legs sucked dry of their contents, corselets of horny armor forever to be unused by any creature, a wing of this insect, the head of that. And dangling by the longest cord of all, with a silken cable wrapped carefully about it to keep the parts together, was the shrunken, shriveled, dried-up body of a long-dead man!

Outside, the nest was a place of gruesome relics. Within, it was a place of luxury and ease. A cushion of softest down filled all the bulging bottom of the hemisphere. A canopy of similarly luxurious texture interposed itself between the rocky roof and the dark, hideous body of the resting spider.

The eyes of the hairy creature glittered like diamonds, even in the darkness, but the loathsome, attenuated legs were tucked under the round-bellied body, and the spider was at rest. It had fed.

It waited, motionless, without desires or aversions, without emotions or perplexities, in comfortable, placid, machinelike contentment until time should bring the call to feed again.

A fresh carcass had been added to the decorations of the nest only the night before. For many days the spider would repose in motionless splendor within the silken castle. When hunger came again, a nocturnal foray, a creature would be pounced upon and slain, brought bodily to the nest, and feasted upon, its body festooned upon the exterior, and another half-sleeping, half-waking period of dreamful idleness within the sybaritic charnel-house would ensue.

Slowly and timidly, half a dozen pink-skinned creatures made their way through the mushroom forest that led to the outcropping of rock under which the clotho spider's nest was slung. They were men, degraded remnants of the once dominant race.

Burl was their leader, and was distinguished solely by two three-foot stumps of the feathery, golden antennæ of a night-flying moth he had bound to his forehead. In his hand was a horny, chitinous spear, taken from the body of an unknown flying creature killed by the flames of the burning purple hills.

Since Burl's return from his solitary—and involuntary—journey, he had been greatly revered by his tribe. Hitherto it had been but a leaderless, formless group of people, creeping to the same hiding-place at nightfall to share in the food of the fortunate, and shudder at the fate of those who might not appear.

Now Burl had walked boldly to them, bearing, upon his back the gray bulk of a labyrinth spider he had slain with his own hands, and clad in wonderful garments of a gorgeousness they envied and admired. They hung upon his words as he struggled to tell them of his adventures, and slowly and dimly they began to look to him for leadership. He was wonderful. For days they had listened breathlessly to the tale of his adventures, but when he demanded that they follow him in another and more perilous affair, they were appalled.

A peculiar strength of will had come to Burl. He had seen and done things that no man in the memory of his tribe had seen or done. He had stood by when the purple hills burned and formed a funeral pyre for the horde of army ants, and for uncounted thousands of flying creatures. He had caught a leaping tarantula upon the point of his spear, and had escaped from the web of a banded web-spider by oiling his body so that the sticky threads of the snare refused to hold him fast. He had attacked and killed a great gray labyrinth spider.

But most potent of all, he had returned and had been welcomed by Saya—Saya of the swift feet and slender limbs, whose smile roused strange emotions in Burl's breast.

It was the adoring gaze of Saya that had roused Burl to this last pitch of rashness. Months before the clotho spider in the hemispherical silk castle of the gruesome decorations had killed and eaten one of the men of the tribe. Burl and the spider's victim had been together when the spider appeared, and the first faint gray light of morning barely silhouetted the shaggy, horrible creature as it leaped from ambush behind a toadstool toward the fear-stricken pair.

Its attenuated legs were outstretched, its mandibles gaped wide, and its jaws clashed horribly as it formed a black blotch in mid air against the lightening sky.

Burl had fled, screaming, when the other man was seized. Now, however, he was leading half a dozen trembling men toward the inverted dome in which the spider dozed. Two or three of them bore spears like Burl himself, but they bore them awkwardly and timorously. Burl himself was possessed by a strange, fictitious courage. It was the utter recklessness of youth, coupled with the eternal masculine desire to display prowess before a desired female.

The wavering advance came to a halt. Most of the naked men stopped from fear, but Burl stopped to invoke his newly discovered inner self, that had furnished him with such marvelous plans. Quite accidentally he had found that if he persistently asked himself a question, some sort of answer came from within.

Now he gazed up from a safe distance and asked himself how he and the others were to slay the clotho spider. The nest was some forty feet from the ground, on the undersurface of a shelf of rock. There was sheer open space beneath it, but it was firmly held to its support by long, silken cables that curled to the upper side of the rock-shelf, clinging to the stone.

Burl gazed, and presently an idea came to him. He beckoned to the others to follow him, and they did so, their knees knocking together from their fright. At the slightest alarm they would flee, screaming in fear, but Burl did not plan that there should be any alarm.

He led them to the rear of the singular rock formation, up the gently sloping side, and toward the precipitous edge. He drew near the point where the rock fell away. A long, tentacle-like silk cable curled up over the edge of a little promontory of stone that jutted out into nothingness.

Burl began to feel oddly cold, and something of the panic of the other men communicated itself to him. This was one of the anchoring cables that held the spider's castle secure. He looked and found others, six or seven in all, which performed the task of keeping the shaggy, horrid ogre's home from falling to the ground below.

His idea did not desert him, however, and he drew back, to whisper orders to his followers. They obeyed him solely because they were afraid, and he spoke in an authoritative tone, but they did obey, and brought a dozen heavy boulders of perhaps forty pounds weight each.

Burl grasped one of the silken cables at its end and tore it loose from the rock for a space of perhaps two yards. His flesh crawled as he did so, but something within him drove him on. Then, while beads of perspiration stood out on his forehead—induced by nothing less than cold, physical fear—he tied the boulder to the cable. The first one done, he felt emboldened, and made a second fast, and a third.

One of his men stood near the edge of the rock, listening in agonized apprehension. Burl had soon tied a heavy stone to each of the cables he saw, and as a matter of fact, there was but one of them he failed to notice. That one had been covered by the flaking mold that took the place of grass upon the rocky eminence.

There were left upon the promontory, several of the boulders for which there was no use, but Burl did not attempt to double the weights on the cables. He took his followers aside and explained his plan in whispers. Quaking, they agreed, and, trembling, they prepared to carry it out.

One of them stationed himself beside each of the boulders, Burl at the largest. He gave a signal, and half a dozen ripping, tearing sounds broke the sullen silence of the day. The boulders clashed and clattered down the rocky side of the precipice, tearing—perhaps "peeling"—the cables from their adhesion to the stone. They shot into open space and jerked violently at the half-globular nest, which was wrenched from its place by the combined impetus of the six heavy weights.

Burl had flung himself upon his face to watch what he was sure would be the death of the spider as it fell forty feet and more, imprisoned in its heavily weighted home. His eyes sparkled with triumph as he saw the ghastly, trophy-laden house swing out from the cliff. Then he gasped in terror.

One of the cables had not been discovered. That single cable held the spider's castle from a fall, though the nest had been torn from its anchorage, and now dangled heavily on its side in mid air. A convulsive struggle seemed to be going on within.

Then one of the archlike doors opened, and the spider emerged, evidently in terror, and confused by the light of day, but still venomous and still deadly. It found but a single of its anchoring cables intact, that leading to the cliff top hard by Burl's head.

The spider sprang for this single cable, and its legs grasped the slender thread eagerly while it began to climb rapidly up toward the cliff top.

As with all the creatures of Burl's time, its first thought was of battle, not flight, and it came up the thin cord with its poison fangs unsheathed and its mandibles clashing in rage. The shaggy hair upon its body seemed to bristle with insane ferocity, and the horrible, thin legs moved with desperate haste as it hastened to meet and wreak vengeance upon the cause of its sudden alarm.

Burl's followers fled, uttering shrieks of fear, and Burl started to his feet, in the grip of a terrible panic. Then his hand struck one of the heavy boulders. Exerting every ounce of his strength, he pushed it over the cliff just where the cable appeared above the edge. For the fraction of a second there was silence, and then the indescribable sound of an impact against a soft body.

There was a gasping cry, and a moment later the curiously muffled clatter of the boulder striking the earth below. Somehow, the sound suggested that the boulder had struck first upon some soft object.

A faint cry came from the bottom of the hill. The last of Burl's men was leaping to a hiding-place among the mushrooms of the forest, and had seen the sheen of shining armor just before him. He cried out and waited for death, but only a delicately formed wasp rose heavily into the air, bearing beneath it the more and more feebly struggling body of a giant cricket.

Burl had stood paralyzed, deprived of the power of movement, after casting the boulder over the cliff. That one action had taken the last ounce of his initiative, and if the spider had hauled itself over the rocky edge and darted toward him, slavering its thick spittle and uttering sounds of mad fury, Burl would not even have screamed as it seized him. He was like a dead thing. But the oddly muffled sound of the boulder striking the ground below brought back hope of life and power of movement.

He peered over the cliff. The nest still dangled at the end of the single cable, still freighted with its gruesome trophies, but on the ground below a crushed and horribly writhing form was moving in convulsions of rage and agony.

Long, hairy legs worked desperately from a body that was no more than a mass of pulped flesh. A ferocious jaw tried to clamp upon something—and there was no other jaw to meet it. An evil-smelling, sticky liquid exuded from the mangled writhing, thing upon the earth, moving in terrible contortions of torment.

Presently an ant drew near and extended inquisitive antennæ at the helpless monster wounded to death. A shrill stridulation sounded out, and three or four other foot-long ants hastened up to wait patiently just outside the spider's reach until its struggles should have lessened enough to make possible the salvage of flesh from the perhaps still-living creature for the ant city a mile away.

And Burl, up on the cliff-top, danced and gesticulated in triumph. He had killed the clotho spider, which had slain one of the tribesmen four months before. Glory was his. All the tribesmen had seen the spider living. Now he would show them the spider dead. He stopped his dance of triumph and walked down the hill in haughty grandeur. He would reproach his timid followers for fleeing from the spider, leaving him to kill it alone.

Quite naïvely Burl assumed that it was his place to give orders and that of the others to obey. True, no one had attempted to give orders before, or to enforce their execution, but Burl had reached the eminently wholesome conclusion that he was a wonderful person whose wishes should be respected.

Burl, filled with fresh notions of his own importance, strutted on toward the hiding-place of the tribe, growing more and more angry with the other men for having deserted him. He would reproach them, would probably beat them. They would be afraid to protest, and in the future would undoubtedly be afraid to run away.

Burl was quite convinced that running away was something he could not tolerate in his followers. Obscurely—and conveniently in the extreme back of his mind—he reasoned that not only did a larger number of men present at a scene of peril increase the chances of coping with the danger, but they also increased the chances that the victim selected by the dangerous creature would be another than himself.

Burl's reasoning was unsophisticated, but sound; perhaps unconscious, but none the less effective. He grew quite furious with the deserters. They had run away! They had fled from a mere spider.

A shrill whine filled the air, and a ten-inch ant dashed at Burl with its mandibles extended threateningly. Burl's path had promised to interrupt the salvaging work of the insect, engaged in scraping shreds of flesh from the corselet of one of the smaller beetles slain the previous night. The ant dashed at Burl like an infuriated fox-terrier, and Burl scurried away in undignified retreat. The ant might not be dangerous, but bites from its formic acid-poisoned mandibles were no trifles.

Burl came to the tangled thicket of mushrooms in which his tribefolk hid. The entrance was tortuous and difficult to penetrate, and could be blocked on occasion with stones and toadstool pulp. Burl made his way toward the central clearing, and heard as he went the sound of weeping, and the excited chatter of the tribes people.

Those who had fled from the rocky cliff had returned with the news that Burl was dead, and Saya lay weeping beneath an over-shadowing toadstool. She was not yet the mate of Burl, but the time would come when all the tribe would recognize a status dimly different from the usual tribal relationship.

Burl stepped into the clearing, and straightway cuffed the first man he came upon, then the next and the next. There was a cry of astonishment, and the next second instinctive, fearful glances at that entrance to the hiding-place.

Had Burl fled from the spider, and was it following? Burl spoke loftily, saying that the spider was dead, that its legs, each one the length of a man, were still, and its fierce jaws and deadly poison-fangs harmless forevermore.

Ten minutes later he was leading an incredulous, awed little group of pink-skinned people to the spot below the cliff where the spider actually lay dead, with the ants busily at work upon its remains.

And when he went back to the hiding-place he donned again his great cloak that was made from the wing of a magnificent moth, slain by the flames of the purple hills, and sat down in splendor upon a crumbling toadstool, to feast upon the glances of admiration and awe that were sent toward him. Only Saya held back shyly, until he motioned for her to draw near, when she seated herself at his feet and gazed up at him with unutterable adoration in her eyes.

But while Burl basked in the radiance of his tribe's admiration, danger was drawing near them all. For many months there had been strange red mushrooms growing slowly here and there all over the earth, they knew. The tribefolk had speculated about them, but forebore tasting them because they were strange, and strange things were usually dangerous and often fatal.

Now those red growths had ripened and grown ready to emit their spores. Their rounded tops had grown fat, and the tough skin grew taut as if a strange pressure were being applied from within. And to-day, while Burl luxuriated in his position of feared and admired great man of his tribe, at a spot a long distance away, upon a hill-top, one of the red mushrooms burst. The spores inside the taut, tough skin shot all about as if scattered by an explosion, and made a little cloud of reddish, impalpable dust, which hung in the air and moved slowly with the sluggish breeze.

A bee droned into the thin red cloud of dust, lazily and heavily flying back toward the hive. But barely had she entered the tinted atmosphere when her movements became awkward and convulsive, effortful and excited. She trembled and twisted in mid air in a peculiar fashion, then dropped to the earth, while her abdomen moved violently.

Bees, like almost all insects, breathe through spiracles on the undersurfaces of their abdomens. This bee had breathed in some of the red mushroom's spores. She thrashed about desperately upon the toadstools on which she had fallen, struggling for breath, for life.

After a long time she was still. The cloud of red mushroom spores had strangled or poisoned her. And everywhere the red fringe grew, such explosions were taking place, one by one, and wherever the red clouds hung in the air creatures were breathing them in and dying in convulsions of strangulation.

THE JOURNEY

Darkness. The soft, blanketing night of the age of fungoids had fallen over all the earth, and there was blackness everywhere that was not good to have. Here and there, however, dim, bluish lights glowed near the ground. There an intermittent glow showed that a firefly had wandered far from the rivers and swamps above which most of his kind now congregated. Now a faintly luminous ball of fire drifted above the steaming, moisture-sodden earth. It was a will-o'-the-wisp, grown to a yard in diameter.

MURRAY LEINSTER

From the low-hanging banks of clouds that hung perpetually overhead, large, warm raindrops fell ceaselessly. A drop, a pause, and then another drop, added to the already dank moisture of the ground below.

The world of fungus growths flourished on just such dampness and humidity. It seemed as if the toadstools and mushrooms could be heard, swelling and growing large in the darkness. Rustlings and stealthy movements sounded furtively through the night, and from above the heavy throb of mighty wing-beats was continuous.

The tribe was hidden in the midst of a tangled copse of toadstools too thickly interwoven for the larger insects to penetrate. Only the little midgets hid in its recesses during the night-time, and the smaller moths during the day.

About and among the bases of the toadstools, however, where their spongy stalks rose from the humid earth, small beetles roamed, singing cheerfully to themselves in deep bass notes. They were small and round, some six or eight inches long, and their bellies were pale gray.

And as they went about they emitted sounds which would have been chirps had they been other than low as the lowest tone of a harp. They were truffle-beetles, in search of the dainty tidbits on which epicures once had feasted.

Some strange sense seemed to tell them when one of half a dozen varieties of truffle was beneath them, and they paused in their wandering to dig a tunnel straight down. A foot, two feet, or two yards, all was the same to them. In time they would come upon the morsel they sought and would remain at the bottom of their temporary home until it was consumed. Then another period of wandering, singing their cheerful song, until another likely spot was reached and another tunnel begun.

In a tiny, open space in the center of the toadstool thicket the tribefolk slept with the deep notes of the truffle-beetles in their ears. A new danger had come to them, but they had passed it on to Burl with a new and childlike confidence and considered the matter settled. They slept, while beneath a glowing mushroom at one side of the clearing Burl struggled with his new problem. He squatted

17

upon the ground in the dim radiance of the shining toadstool, his moth-wing cloak wrapped about him, his spear in his hand, and his twin golden plumes of the moth's antennæ bound to his forehead. But his face was downcast as a child's.

The red mushrooms had begun to burst. Only that day, one of the women, seeking edible fungus for the tribal larder, had seen the fat, distended globule of the red mushroom. Its skin was stretched taut, and glistened in the light.

The woman paid little or no attention to the red growth. Her ears were attuned to catch sounds that would warn her of danger while her eyes searched for tidbits that would make a meal for the tribe, and more particularly for her small son, left behind at the hiding-place.

A ripping noise made her start up, alert on the instant. The red envelope of the mushroom had split across the top, and a thick cloud of brownish-red dust was spurting in every direction. It formed a pyramidal cloud some thirty feet in height, which enlarged and grew thinner with minor eddies within itself.

A little yellow butterfly with wings barely a yard from tip to tip, flapped lazily above the mushroom-covered plain. Its wings beat the air with strokes that seemed like playful taps upon a friendly element. The butterfly was literally intoxicated with the sheer joy of living. It had emerged from its cocoon barely two hours before, and was making its maiden flight above the strange and wonderful world. It fluttered carelessly into the red-brown cloud of mushroom spores.

The woman was watching the slowly changing form of the spore-mist. She saw the butterfly enter the brownish dust, and then her eyes became greedy. There was something the matter with the butterfly. Its wings no longer moved lazily and gently. They struck out in frenzied, hysterical blows that were erratic and wild. The little yellow creature no longer floated lightly and easily, but dashed here and there, wildly and without purpose, seeming to be in its death-throes.

It crashed helplessly against the ground and lay there, moving feebly. The woman hurried forward. The wings would be new fabric with which to adorn herself, and the fragile legs of the butterfly contained choice meat. She entered the dust-cloud.

MURRAY LEINSTER

A stream of intolerable fire—though the woman had never seen or known of fire—burned her nostrils and seared her lungs. She gasped in pain, and the agony was redoubled. Her eyes smarted as if burning from their sockets, and tears blinded her.

The woman instinctively turned about to flee, but before she had gone a dozen yards—blinded as she was—she stumbled and fell to the ground. She lay there, gasping, and uttering moans of pain, until one of the men of the tribe who had been engaged in foraging near by saw her and tried to find what had injured her.

She could not speak, and he was about to leave her and tell the other tribefolk about her when he heard the clicking of an ant's limbs, and rather than have the ant pick her to pieces bit by bit—and leave his curiosity ungratified—the man put her across his shoulders and bore her back to the hiding-place of the tribe.

It was the tale the woman had told when she partly recovered that caused Burl to sit alone all that night beneath the shining toadstool in the little clearing, puzzling his just-awakened brain to know what to do.

The year before there had been no red mushrooms. They had appeared only recently, but Burl dimly remembered that one day, a long time before, there had been a strange breeze which blew for three day and nights, and that during the time of its blowing all the tribe had been sick and had wept continually.

Burl had not yet reached the point of mental development when he would associate that breeze with a storm at a distance, or reason that the spores of the red mushrooms had been borne upon the wind to the present resting-places of the deadly fungus growths. Still less could he decide that the breeze had not been deadly only because it was lightly laden with the fatal dust.

He knew simply that unknown red mushrooms had appeared, that they were everywhere about, and that they would burst, and that to breathe the red dust they gave out was grievous sickness or death.

The tribe slept while the bravely attired figure of Burl squatted under the glowing disk of the luminous mushroom, his face a picture of querulous perplexity, and his heart full of sadness.

He had consulted his strange inner self, and no plan had come to

19

him. He knew the red mushrooms were all about. They would fill the air with their poison. He struggled with his problem while his people slumbered, and the woman who had breathed the mushroom-dust sobbed softly in her troubled sleep.

Presently a figure stirred on the farther side of the clearing. Saya woke and raised her head. She saw Burl crouching by the shining toadstool, his gay attire draggled and unnoticed. She watched him for a little, and the desolation of his pose awoke her pity.

She rose and went to his side, taking his hand between her two, while she spoke his name softly. When he turned and looked at her, confusion smote her, but the misery in his face brought confidence again.

Burl's sorrow was inarticulate—he could not explain this new responsibility for his people that had come to him—but he was comforted by her presence, and she sat down beside him. After a long time she slept, with her head resting against his side, but he continued to question himself, continued to demand an escape for his people from the suffering and danger he saw ahead. With the day an answer came.

When Burl had been carried down the river on his fungus raft, and had landed in the country of the army ants, he had seen great forests of edible mushrooms, and had said to himself that he would bring Saya to that place. He remembered, now, that the red mushrooms were there also, but the idea of a journey remained.

The hunting-ground of his tribe had been free of the red fungoids until recently. If he traveled far enough he would come to a place where there were still no red toadstools. Then came the decision. He would lead his tribe to a far country.

He spoke with stern authority when the tribesmen woke, talking in few words and in a loud voice, holding up his spear as he gave his orders.

The timid, pink-skinned people obeyed him meekly. They had seen the body of the clotho spider he had slain, and he had thrown down before them the gray bulk of the labyrinth spider he had thrust through with his spear. Now he was to take them through unknown dangers to an unknown haven, but they feared to displease him.

They made light loads of their mushrooms and such meat-stuffs as they had, and parceled out what little fabric they still possessed. Three men bore spears, in addition to Burl's long shaft, and he had persuaded the other three to carry clubs, showing them how the weapon should be wielded.

The indefinitely brighter spot in the cloud-banks above that meant the shining sun had barely gone a quarter of the way across the sky when the trembling band of timid creatures made their way from their hiding-place and set out upon their journey. For their course, Burl depended entirely upon chance. He avoided the direction of the river, however, and the path along which he had returned to his people. He knew the red mushrooms grew there. Purely by accident he set his march toward the west, and walked cautiously on, his tribesfolk following him fearfully.

Burl walked ahead, his spear held ready. He made a figure at once brave and pathetic, venturing forth in a world of monstrous ferocity and incredible malignance, armed only with a horny spear borrowed from a dead insect. His velvety cloak, made from a moth's wing, hung about his figure in graceful folds, however, and twin golden plumes nodded jauntily from his forehead.

Behind him the nearly naked people followed reluctantly. Here a woman with a baby in her arms, there children of nine or ten, unable to resist the Instinct to play even in the presence of the manifold dangers of the march. They ate hungrily of the lumps of mushroom they had been ordered to carry. Then a long-legged boy, his eyes roving anxiously about in search of danger followed.

Thirty thousand years of flight from every peril had deeply submerged the combative nature of humanity. After the boy came two men, one with a short spear, and the other with a club, each with a huge mass of edible mushroom under his free arm, and both badly frightened at the idea of fleeing from dangers they knew and feared to dangers they did not know and consequently feared much more.

So was the caravan spread out. It made its way across the country with many deviations from a fixed line, and with many halts and pauses. Once a shrill stridulation filled all the air before them, a monster sound compounded of innumerable clickings and high-pitched cries.

They came to the tip of an eminence and saw a great space of ground covered with tiny black bodies locked in combat. For quite half a mile in either direction the earth was black with ants, snapping and biting at each other, locked in vise-like embraces, each combatant couple trampled under the feet of the contending armies, with no thought of surrender or quarter.

The sound of the clashing of fierce jaws upon horny armor, the cries of the maimed, and strange sounds made by the dying, and above all, the whining battle-cry of each of the fighting hordes, made a sustained uproar that was almost deafening.

From either side of the battle-ground a pathway led back to separate ant-cities, a pathway marked by the hurrying groups of reinforcements rushing to the fight. Tiny as the ants were, for once no lumbering beetle swaggered insolently in their path, nor did the hunting-spiders mark them out for prey. Only little creatures smaller than the combatants themselves made use of the insect war for purposes of their own.

These were little gray ants barely more than four inches long, who scurried about in and among the fighting creatures with marvelous dexterity, carrying off, piece-meal, the bodies of the dead, and slaying the wounded for the same fate.

They hung about the edges of the battle, and invaded the abandoned areas when the tide of battle shifted, insect guerrillas, fighting for their own hands, careless of the origin of the quarrel, espousing no cause, simply salvaging the dead and living débris of the combat.

Burl and his little group of followers had to make a wide detour to avoid the battle itself, and the passage between bodies of reinforcements hurrying to the scene of strife was a matter of some difficulty. The ants running rapidly toward the battle-field were hugely excited. Their antennæ waved wildly, and the infrequent wounded one, limping back toward the city, was instantly and repeatedly challenged by the advancing insects.

They crossed their antennæ upon his, and required thorough

evidence that he was of the proper city before allowing him to proceed. Once they arrived at the battle-field they flung themselves into the fray, becoming lost and indistinguishable in the tide of straining, fighting black bodies.

Men in such a battle, without distinguishing marks or battle-cries, would have fought among themselves as often as against their foes, but the ants had a much simpler method of identification. Each ant-city possesses its individual odor—a variant on the scent of formic acid—and each individual of that city is recognized in his world quite simply and surely by the way he smells.

The little tribe of human beings passed precariously behind a group of a hundred excited insect warriors, and before the following group of forty equally excited black insects. Burl hurried on with his following, putting many miles of perilous territory behind before nightfall. Many times during the day they saw the sudden billowing of a red-brown dust-cloud from the earth, and more than once they came upon the empty skin and drooping stalk of one of the red mushrooms, and more often still they came upon the mushrooms themselves, grown fat and taut, prepared to send their deadly spores into the air when the pressure from within became more than the leathery skin could stand.

That night the tribe hid among the bases of giant puff-balls, which at a touch shot out a puff of white powder resembling smoke. The powder was precisely the same in nature as that cast out by the red mushrooms, but its effects were marvelously—and mercifully—different; it was innocuous.

Burl slept soundly this night, having been two days and a night without rest, but the remainder of his tribe, and even Saya, were fearful and afraid, listening ceaselessly all through the dark hours for the menacing sounds of creatures coming to prey upon them.

And so for a week the march kept on. Burl would not allow his tribe to stop to forage for food. The red mushrooms were all about. Once one of the little children was caught in a whirling eddy of red dust, and its mother rushed into the deadly stuff to seize it and bring it out. Then the tribe had to hide for three days while the two of them recovered from the debilitating poison.

THE RED DUST

Once, too, they found a half-acre patch of the giant cabbages—there were six of them full grown, and a dozen or more smaller ones—and Burl took two men and speared two of the huge, twelve-foot slugs that fed upon the leaves. When the tribe passed on it was gorged on the fat meat of the slugs, and there was much soft fur, so that all the tribefolk wore loin-cloths of the yellow stuff.

There were perils, too, in the journey. On the fourth day of the tribe's traveling, Burl froze suddenly into stillness. One of the hairy tarantulas—a trap-door spider with a black belly—had fallen upon a scarabæus beetle, and was devouring it only a hundred yards ahead.

The tribefolk, trembling, went back for half a mile or more in panic-stricken silence, and refused to advance until he had led them a detour of two or three miles to one side of the dangerous spot.

Long, fear-ridden marches through perilous countries unknown to them, through the golden aisles of yellow mushroom forests, over the flaking surfaces of plains covered with many-colored "rusts" and molds; pauses beside turbid pools whose waters were concealed by thick layers of green slime, and other evil-smelling ponds which foamed and bubbled slowly, which were covered with pasty yeasts that rose in strange forms of discolored foam.

Fleeting glimpses they had of the glistening spokes of symmetrical spiders'-webs, whose least thread it would have been beyond the power of the strongest of the tribe to break. They passed through a forest of puff-balls, which boomed when touched and shot a puff of vapor from their open mouths.

Once they saw a long and sinuous insect that fled before them and disappeared into a burrow in the ground, running with incredible speed upon legs of uncountable number. It was a centipede all of thirty feet in length, and when they crossed the path it had followed a horrible stench came to their nostrils so that they hurried on.

Long escape from unguessed dangers brought boldness, of a sort, to the pink-skinned men, and they would have rested. They went to Burl with their complaint, and he simply pointed with his hands behind them. There were three little clouds of brownish vapor in the air, where they could see, along the road they had traversed. To the right of them a dust-cloud was just settling, and to the left another rose as they looked.

A new trick of the deadly dust became apparent now. Toward the end of a day in which they had traveled a long distance, one of the little children ran a little to the left of the route its elders were following. The earth had taken on a brownish hue, and the child stirred up the surface mould with its feet.

The brownish dust that had settled there was raised again, and the child ran, crying and choking, to its mother, its lungs burning as with fire, and its eyes like hot coals. Another day would pass before the child could walk.

In a strange country, knowing nothing of the dangers that might assail the tribe while waiting for the child to recover, Burl looked about for a hiding-place. Far over to the right a low cliff, perhaps twenty or thirty feet high, showed sides of crumbling, yellow clay, and from where Burl stood he could see the dark openings of burrows scattered here and there upon its face.

He watched for a time, to see if any bee or wasp inhabited them, knowing that many kinds of both insects dig burrows for their young, and do not occupy them themselves. No dark forms appeared, however, and he led his people toward the openings.

The appearance of the holes confirmed his surmise. They had been dug months before by mining bees, and the entrances were "weathered" and worn. The tribefolk made their way into the three-foot tunnels, and hid themselves, seizing the opportunity to gorge themselves upon the food they carried.

Burl stationed himself near the outer end of one of the little caves to watch for signs of danger. While waiting he poked curiously with his spear at a little pile of white and sticky parchment-like stuff he saw just within the mouth of the tunnel.

Instantly movement became visible. Fifty, sixty, or a hundred tiny creatures, no more than half an inch in length, tumbled pell-mell from the dirty-white heap. Awkward legs, tiny, greenish-black bodies, and bristles protruding in every direction made them strange to look upon.

They had tumbled from the whitish heap and now they made haste to hide themselves in it again, moving slowly and clumsily, with immense effort and laborious contortions of their bodies.

Burl had never seen any insect progress in such a slow and ineffective fashion before. He drew one little insect back with the point of his spear and examined it from a safe distance. Tiny jaws before the head met like twin sickles, and the whole body was shaped like a rounded diamond lozenge.

Burl knew that no insect of such small size could be dangerous, and leaned over, then took one creature in his hand. It wriggled frantically and slipped from his fingers, dropping upon the soft yellow caterpillar-fur he had about his middle. Instantly, as if it were a conjuring trick, the little insect vanished, and Burl searched for a matter of minutes before he found it hidden deep in the long, soft hairs of the fur, resting motionless, and evidently at ease.

It was a bee-louse, the first larval form of a beetle whose horny armor could be seen in fragments for yards before the clayey cliff-side. Hidden in the openings of the bee's tunnel, it waited until the bee-grubs farther back in their separate cells should complete their changes of form and emerge into the open air, passing over the cluster of tiny creatures at the doorway. As the bees pass, the little bee-lice would clamber in eager haste up their hairy legs and come to rest in the fur about their thoraxes. Then, weeks later, when the bees in turn made other cells and stocked them with honey for the eggs they would lay, the tiny creatures would slip from their resting-places and be left behind in the fully provisioned cell, to eat not only the honey the bee had so laboriously acquired, but the very grub hatched from the bee's egg.

Burl had no difficulty in detaching the small insect and casting it away, but in doing so discovered three more that had hidden themselves in his furry garment, no doubt thinking it the coat of their natural, though unwilling hosts. He plucked them away, and discovered more, and more. His garment was the hiding-place for dozens of the creatures.

Disgusted and annoyed, he went out of the cavern and to a spot some distance away, where he took off his robe and pounded it with the flat side of his spear to dislodge the visitors. They dropped out one by one, reluctantly, and finally the garment was clean of them.

Then Burl heard a shout from the direction of the mining-bee caves, and hastened toward the sound.

It was then drawing toward the time of darkness, but one of the tribesmen had ventured out and found no less than three of the great imperial mushrooms. Of the three, one had been attacked by a parasitic purple mould, but the gorgeous yellow of the other two was undimmed, and the people were soon feasting upon the firm flesh.

Burl felt a little pang of jealousy, though he joined in the consumption of the find as readily as the others, and presently drew a little to one side.

He cast his eyes across the country, level and unbroken as far as the eye could see. The small clay cliff was the only inequality visible, and its height cut off all vision on one side. But the view toward the horizon was unobstructed on three sides, and here and there the black speck of a monster bee could be seen, droning homeward to its hive or burrow, and sometimes the slender form of a wasp passed overhead, its transparent wings invisible from the rapidity of their vibrations.

These flew high in the air, but lower down, barely skimming the tops of the many-colored mushrooms and toadstools, fluttering lightly above the swollen fungoids, and touching their dainty proboscides to unspeakable things in default of the fragrant flowers that were normal food for their races—lower down flew the multitudes of butterflies the age of mushrooms had produced.

White and yellow and red and brown, pink and blue and purple and green, every shade and every color, every size and almost every shape, they flitted gaily in the air. There were some so tiny that they would barely have shaded Burl's face, and some beneath whose slender bodies he could have hidden himself. They flew in a riot of colors and tints above a world of foul mushroom growths, and turgid, slime-covered ponds.

Burl, temporarily out of the limelight because of the discovery of a store of food by another member of the tribe, bethought himself of an idea. Soon night would come on, the cloud-bank would turn red in the west, and then darkness would lean downward from the sky. With the coming of that time these creatures of the day would seek hiding-places, and the air would be given over to the furry moths that flew by night. He, Burl, would mark the spot where one of the larger creatures alighted, and would creep up upon it, with his spear held fast.

His wide blue eyes brightened at the thought, and he sat himself down to watch. After a long time the soft, down-reaching fingers of the night touched the shaded aisles of the mushroom forests, and a gentle haze arose above the golden glades. One by one the gorgeous fliers of the daytime dipped down and furled their painted wings. The overhanging clouds became darker—finally black, and the slow, deliberate rainfall that lasted all through the night began. Burl rose and crept away into the darkness, his spear held in readiness.

Through the black night, beneath deeper blacknesses which were the dark undersides of huge toadstools, creeping silently, with every sense alert for sign of danger or for hope of giant prey, Burl made his slow advance.

A glorious butterfly of purple and yellow markings, whose wings spread out for three yards on either side of its delicately formed body, had hidden itself barely two hundred yards away. Burl could imagine it, now, preening its slender limbs and combing from its long and slender proboscis any trace of the delectable foodstuffs on which it had fed during the day. Burl moved slowly and cautiously forward, all eyes and ears.

He heard an indescribable sound in a thicket a little to his left, and shifted his course. The sound was the faint whistling of air through the breathing-holes along an insect's abdomen. Then came the delicate rustling of filmy wings being stretched and closed again, and the movement of sharply barbed feet upon the soft earth. Burl moved in breathless silence, holding his spear before him in readiness to plunge it into the gigantic butterfly's soft body.

The mushrooms here were grown thickly together, so there was no room for Burl's body to pass between their stalks, and the rounded heads were deformed and misshapen from their crowdings. Burl spent precious moments in trying to force a silent passage, but had to own himself beaten. Then he clambered up upon the spongy mass of mushroom heads, trusting to luck that they would sustain his weight.

The blackness was intense, so that even the forms of objects before him were lost in obscurity. He moved forward for some ten yards, however, walking gingerly over his precarious foothold. Then he felt rather than saw the opening before him. A body moved below him.

Burl raised his spear, and with a yell plunged down on the back of the moving thing, thrusting his spear with all the force he could command. He landed on a shifting form, but his yell of triumph turned to a scream of terror.

This was not the yielding body of a slender butterfly that he had come upon, nor had his spear penetrated the creature's soft flesh. He had fallen upon the shining back of one of the huge, meat-eating beetles, and his spear had slid across the horny armor, and then stuck fast, having pierced only the leathery tissue between the insect's head and thorax.

Burl's terror was pitiable at the realization, but as nothing to the ultimate panic which possessed him when the creature beneath him uttered a grunt of fright and pain, and, spreading its stiff wing-cases wide, shot upward in a crazy, panic-stricken, rocket-like flight toward the sky.

THE SEXTON-BEETLES

Burl fell headforemost upon the spongy top of a huge toadstool that split with the impact and let him through to the ground beneath, powdering him with its fine spores. He came to rest with his naked shoulder half-way through the yielding flesh of a mushroom-stalk, and lay there for a second, catching his breath to scream again.

Then he heard the whining buzz of his attempted prey. There was something wrong with the beetle. Burl's spear had struck it in an awkward spot, and it was rocketing upward in erratic flight that ended in a crash two or three hundreds yards away.

Burl sprang up in an instant. Perhaps, despite his mistake, he had slain this infinitely more worthy victim. He rushed toward the spot where it had fallen.

His wide blue eyes pierced the darkness well enough to enable him to sheer off from masses of toadstools, but he could distinguish no details—nothing but forms. He heard the beetle floundering upon the ground; then heard it mount again into the air, more clumsily than before.

Its wing-beats no longer kept up a sustained note. They thrashed the air irregularly and wildly. The flight was zigzag and uncertain, and though longer than the first had been, it ended similarly, in a heavy fall. Another period of floundering, and the beetle took to the air again just before Burl arrived at the spot.

It was obviously seriously hurt, and Burl forgot the dangers of the night in his absorption in the chase. He darted after his prey, fleet-footed and agile, taking chances that in cold blood he would never have thought of.

Twice, in the pain-racked struggles of the monster beetle, he arrived at the spot where the gigantic insect flung itself about madly, insanely, fighting it knew not what, striking out with colossal wings and legs, dazed and drunk with agony. And each time it managed to get aloft in flight that was weaker and more purposeless.

Crazy, fleeing from the torturing spear that pierced its very vitals, the beetle blundered here and there, floundering among the mushroom thickets in spasms that were constantly more prolonged and more agonized, but nevertheless flying heavily, lurching drunkenly, managing to graze the tops of the toadstools in one more despairing, tormented flight.

And Burl followed, aflame with the fire of the chase, arriving at the scene of each successive, panic-stricken struggle on the ground just after the beetle had taken flight again, but constantly more closely on the heels of the weakening monster.

At last he came up panting, and found the giant lying upon the earth, moving feebly, apparently unable to rise. How far he was from the tribe, Burl did not know, nor did the question occur to him at the moment. He waited for the beetle to be still, trembling with excitement and eagerness. The struggles of the huge form grew more feeble, and at last ceased. Burl moved forward and grasped his spear. He wrenched at it to thrust again.

In an instant the beetle had roused itself, and was exerting its last atom of strength, galvanized into action by the agony caused by Burl's seizure of the spear. A great wing-cover knocked Burl twenty feet, and flung him against the base of a mushroom, where he lay, half stunned. But then a strangely pungent scent came to his nostrils—the scent of the red mushrooms!

He staggered to his feet and fled, while behind him the gigantic beetle crashed and floundered—Burl heard a tearing and ripping sound. The insect had torn the covering of one of the red mushrooms, tightly packed with the fatal red dust. At the noise, Burl's speed was doubled, but he could still hear the frantic struggles of the dying beetle grow to a very crescendo of desperation.

The creature broke free and managed to rise in a final flight, fighting for breath and life, weakened and tortured by the spear and the horrible spores of the red mushrooms. Then it crashed suddenly to the earth and was still. The red dust had killed it.

In time to come, Burl might learn to use the red dust as poison gas had been used by his ancestors of thirty thousand years before, but now he was frightened and alone, lost from his tribe, and with no faintest notion of how to find them. He crouched beneath a huge toadstool and waited for dawn, listening with terrified apprehension for the ripping sound that would mean the bursting of another of the red mushrooms.

Only the wing beats of night-flying creatures came to his ears, however, and the discordant noises of the four-foot truffle-beetles as they roamed the aisles of the mushroom forests, seeking the places beneath which their instinct told them fungoid dainties awaited the courageous miner. The eternal dripping of the raindrops falling at long intervals from the overhanging clouds formed a soft obbligato to the whole.

Burl listened, knowing there were red toadstools all about, but not once during the whole of the long, dark hours did the rending noise tell of a bursting fungus casting loose its freight of deadly dust upon the air. Only when day came again, and the chill dampness of the night was succeeded by the steaming humidity of the morning, did a tall pyramid of brownish-red stuff leap suddenly into the air from a ripped mushroom covering.

Then Burl stood up and looked around. Here and there, all over the whole countryside, slowly and at intervals, the cones of fatal red sprang into the air. Had Burl lived thirty thousand years earlier, he

31

might have likened the effect to that of shells bursting from a leisurely bombardment, but as it was he saw in them only fresh and inexorable dangers added to an already peril-ridden existence.

A hundred yards from where he had hidden during the night the body of his victim lay, crumpled up and limp. Burl approached speculatively. He had come even before the ants appeared to take their toll of the carcass, and not even a buzzing flesh-fly had placed its maggots on the unresisting form.

The long, whiplike antennæ lay upon the carpet of mold and rust, and the fiercely toothed legs were drawn close against the body. The many-faceted eyes stared unseeingly, and the stiff and horny wing-cases were rent and torn.

When Burl went to the other side of the dead beetle he saw something that filled him with elation. His spear had been held between his body and the beetle's during that mad flight, and at the final crash, when Burl shot away from the fear-crazed insect, the weight of his body had forced the spearpoint between the joints of the corselet and the neck. Even if the red dust had not finished the creature, the spear wound in time would have ended its life.

Burl was thrilled once more by his superlative greatness, and conveniently forgot that it was the red dust that had actually administered the *coup de grâce*. It was so much more pleasant to look upon himself as the mighty slayer that he hacked off one of the barb-edged limbs to carry back to his tribe in evidence of his feat. He took the long antennæ, too, as further proof.

Then he remembered that he did not know where his tribe was to be found. He had no faintest idea of the direction in which the beetle had flown. As a matter of fact, the course of the beetle had been in turn directed toward every point of the compass, and there was no possible way of telling the relation of its final landing-place to the point from which it had started.

Burl wrestled with his problem for an hour, and then gave up in disgust. He set off at random, with the leg of the huge insect flung over his shoulder and the long antennæ clasped in his hand with his spear. He turned to look at his victim of the night before just before plunging into the near-by mushroom forest, and saw that it was already the center of a mass of tiny black bodies, pulling and hacking at the tough armor, and carving out great lumps of the succulent flesh to be carried to the near-by ant city.

In the teeming life of the insect world death is an opportunity for the survivors. There is a strangely tense and fearful competition for the bodies of the slain. There had been barely an hour of daylight in which the ants might seek for provender, yet in that little time the freshly killed beetle had been found and was being skilfully and carefully exploited. When the body of one of the larger insects fell to the ground, there was a mighty rush, a fierce race, among all the tribes of scavengers to see who should be first.

Usually the ants had come upon the scene and were inquisitively exploring the carcass long before even the flesh-flies had arrived, who dropped their living maggots upon the creature. The blue-bottles came still later, to daub their masses of white eggs about the delicate membranes of the eye.

And while all the preceding scavengers were at work, furtive beetles and tiny insects burrowed below the reeking body to attack the highly scented flesh from a fresh angle.

Each working independently of the others, they commonly appeared in the order of the delicacy of the sense which could lead them to a source of food, though accident could and sometimes did afford one group of workers in putrescence an advantage over the others.

Thus, sometimes a blue-bottle anticipated even the eager ants, and again the very flesh-flies dropped their squirming offspring upon a limp form that was already being undermined by white-bellied things working in the darkness below the body.

Burl grimaced at the busy ants and buzzing flies, and disappeared into the mushroom forest. Here for a long time he moved cautiously and silently through the aisles of tangled stalks and the spongy, round heads of the fungoids. Now and then he saw one of the red toadstools, and made a wide detour around it. Twice they burst within his sight, circumscribed as his vision was by the toadstools among which he was traveling.

Each time he ran hastily to put as much distance as possible

33

between himself and the deadly red dust. He traveled for an hour or more, looking constantly for familiar landmarks that might guide him to his tribe. He knew that if he came upon any place he had seen while with his tribe he could follow the path they had traveled and in time rejoin them.

For many hours he went on, alert for signs of danger. He was quite ignorant of the fact that there were such things as points of the compass, and though he had a distinct notion that he was not moving in a straight line, he did not realize that he was actually moving in a colossal half-circle. After walking steadily for nearly four hours he was no more than three miles in a direct line from his starting-point. As it happened, his uncertainty of direction was fortunate.

The night before the tribe had been feeding happily upon one of the immense edible mushrooms, when they heard Burl's abruptly changing cry. It had begun as a shout of triumph, and ended as a scream of fear. Then they heard hurried wing-beats as a creature rose into the air in a scurry of desperation. The throbbing of huge wings ended in a heavy fall, followed by another flight.

Velvety darkness masked the sky, and the tribesmen could only stare off into the blackness, where their leader had vanished, and begin to tremble, wondering what they should do in a strange country with no bold chief to guide them.

He was the first man to whom the tribe had ever offered allegiance, but their submission had been all the more complete for that fact, and his loss was the more appalling.

Burl had mistaken their lack of timidity. He had thought it independence, and indifference to him. As a matter of fact, it was security because the tribe felt safe under his tutelage. Now that he had vanished, and in a fashion that seemed to mean his death, their old fears returned to them reenforced by the strangeness of their surroundings.

They huddled together and whispered their fright to one another, listening the while in panic-stricken apprehension for signs of danger. The tribesmen visualized Burl caught in fiercely toothed limbs, being rent and torn in mid air by horny, insatiable jaws, his blood falling in great spurts toward the earth below. They caught a faint, reedy cry, and shuddered, pressing closer together.

And so through the long night they waited in trembling silence. Had a hunting spider appeared among them they would not have lifted a hand to defend themselves, but would have fled despairingly, would probably have scattered and lost touch with one another, and spent the remainder of their lives as solitary fugitives, snatching fear-ridden rest in strange hiding-places.

But day came again, and they looked into each other's eyes, reading in each the selfsame panic and fear. Saya was probably the most pitiful of all the group. Burl was to have been her mate, and her face was white and drawn beyond that of any of the rest of the tribefolk.

With the day, they did not move, but remained clustered about the huge mushroom on which they had been feeding the night before. They spoke in hushed and fearful tones, huddled together, searching all the horizon for insect enemies. Saya would not eat, but sat still, staring before her in unseeing indifference. Burl was dead.

A hundred yards from where they crouched a red mushroom glistened in the pale light of the new day. Its tough skin was taut and bulging, resisting the pressure of the spores within. But slowly, as the morning wore on, some of the moisture that had kept the skin soft and flaccid during the night evaporated.

The skin had a strong tendency to contract, like green leather when drying. The spores within it strove to expand. The opposing forces produced a tension that grew greater and greater as more and more of the moisture was absorbed by the air. At last the skin could hold no longer.

With a ripping sound that could be heard for hundreds of feet, the tough wrapping split and tore across its top, and with a hollow, booming noise the compressed mass of deadly spores rushed into the air, making a pyramidal cloud of brown-red dust some sixty feet in height.

The tribesmen quivered at the noise and faced the dust cloud for a fleeting instant, then ran pell-mell to escape the slowly moving tide of death as the almost imperceptible breeze wafted it slowly toward them. Men and women, boys and girls, they fled in a mad rush from the deadly stuff, not pausing to see that even as it advanced it settled slowly to the ground, nor stopping to observe its path that they might step aside and let it go safely by.

Saya fled with the rest, but without their extreme panic. She fled because the others had done so, and ran more carelessly, struggling with a half-formed idea that it did not particularly matter whether she were caught or not.

She fell slightly behind the others, without being noticed. Then quite abruptly a stone turned under her foot, and she fell headlong, striking her head violently against a second stone. Then she lay quite still while the red cloud billowed slowly toward her, drifting gently in the faint, hardly perceptible breeze.

It drew nearer and nearer, settling slowly, but still a huge and menacing mass of deadly dust. It gradually flattened out, too, so that though it had been a rounded cone at first, it flowed over the minor inequalities of the ground as a huge and tenuous leech might have crawled, sucking from all breathing creatures the life they had within them.

A hundred and fifty yards away, a hundred yards away, then only fifty yards away. From where Saya lay unconscious on the earth, eddies within the moving mass could be seen, and the edges took on a striated appearance, telling of the curling of the dust wreaths in the larger mass of deadly powder.

The deliberate advance kept on, seeming almost purposeful. It would have seemed possible to draw from the unhurried, menacing movement of the poisonous stuff that some malign intelligence was concealed in it, that it was, in fact, a living creature. But when the misty edges of the cloud were no more than twenty-five yards from Saya's prostrate body a breeze from one side sprang up—a vagrant, fitful little breeze, that first halted the red cloud and threw it into confusion and then drove it to one side, so that it passed Saya without harming her, though a single trailing wisp of dark-red mist floated very close to her.

Then for a time Saya lay still indeed, only her breast rising and falling gently with faint and irregular breaths. Her head had struck a sharp-edged stone in her fall, and a tiny pool of sticky red had gathered from the wound.

Perhaps thirty feet from where she lay, three small toadstools grew in a little clump, their bases so close together that they seemed but one. From between two of them, however, just where they parted, twin tufts of reddish threads appeared, twinkling back and forth, and in and out. As if they had given some reassuring sign, two slender antennæ followed, then bulging eyes, and then a small black body which had bright-red scalloped markings upon the wing-cases.

It was a tiny beetle no more than eight inches long—a burying-beetle. It drew near Saya's body and clambered upon her, explored the ground by her side, moving all the time in feverish haste, and at last dived into the ground beneath her shoulder, casting back a little shower of hastily dug earth as it disappeared.

Ten minutes later another similar insect appeared, and upon the heels of the second a third. Each of them made the same hasty examination, and each dived under the still form. Presently the earth seemed to billow at a spot along Saya's side, then at another. Perhaps ten minutes after the arrival of the third beetle a little rampart had reared itself all about Saya's body, precisely following the outline of her form. Then her body moved slightly, in a number of tiny jerks, and seemed to settle perhaps half an inch into the ground.

The burying beetles were of those who exploited the bodies of the fallen. Working from below, they excavated the earth from the under side of such prizes as they came upon, then turned upon their backs and thrust with their legs, jerking the body so it sank into the shallow excavation they had prepared.

The process would be repeated until at last the whole of the gift of fortune had sunk below the surrounding surface and the loosened earth fell in upon the top, thus completing the inhumation.

Then in the darkness the beetles would feast and rear their young, gorging upon the plentiful supply of succulent foodstuff they had hidden from jealous fellow scavengers above them.

But Saya was alive. Thirty thousand years before, when scientists examined into the habits of the burying-beetles, or the sexton-beetles, they had declared that fresh meat or living meat would not be touched. They based their statement solely upon the fact that the insects (then tiny creatures indeed) did not appear until the trap-meat placed by the investigators had remained untouched for days.

Conditions had changed in thirty thousand years. The ever-present ants and the sharp-eyed flies were keen rivals of the brightly arrayed beetles. Usually the tribes of creatures who worked in the darkness below ground came after the ants had taken their toll, and the flies sipped daintily.

When Saya fell unconscious upon the ground, however, it was the one accident that caused the burying-beetle to find her first, before the ants had come to tear the flesh from her slender, soft-skinned body. She breathed gently and irregularly, her face drawn with the sorrow of the night before, while desperately hurrying beetles swarmed beneath her body, channeling away the earth so that she would sink lower and lower into the ground.

An inch, and a long wait. Then she sank slowly a second inch. The bright-red tufts of thread appeared again, and a beetle made his way to the open air. He moved hastily about, inspecting the progress of the work. He dived below again. Another inch, and after a long time another inch was excavated.

Burl stepped out from a group of over-shadowing toadstools and halted. He cast his eyes over the landscape, and was struck by its familiarity. It was, in point of fact, very near the spot he had left the night before, in pursuit of a colossal wounded beetle.

Burl moved back and forth, trying to account for the sensation of recognition, and then trying to approximate the place from which he had last seen it.

He passed within fifty feet of the spot where Saya lay, now half buried in the ground. The loose earth cast up about her body had begun to fall in little rivulets upon her. One of her shoulders was already screened from view.

Burl passed on, unseeing. He was puzzling over the direction from which he had seen the particular section of countryside before him. Perhaps a little farther on he would come to the place. He hurried a little. In a moment he recognized his location. There was the great edible mushroom, half broken away, from which the tribe had been feeding. There were the mining bee burrows.

His feet stirred up a fine dust, and he stopped short. A red mushroom had covered the earth with a thin layer of its impalpable, deadly powder. Burl understood why the tribe had gone, and a cold sweat came upon his body. Was Saya safe, or had the whole tribe succumbed to the poisonous stuff? Had they all, men and women and children, died in convulsions of gasping strangulation?

He hurried to retrace his footsteps. There was a fragment of mushrooms on the ground. Here was a spear, cast away by one of the tribesmen in his flight. Burl broke into a run.

The little excavation into which Saya was sinking, inch by inch, was all of twenty-five feet to the right of the path. Burl dashed on, frantic with anxiety about the tribe, but most of all about Saya. Saya's body quivered and sank a fraction more into the earth.

Half a dozen little rivulets of dirt were tumbling upon her body now. In a matter of minutes she would be hidden from view. Burl ran madly past her, too busy searching the mushroom thickets before him with his eyes to dream of looking upon the ground.

Twenty yards from a huge toadstool thicket a noise arrested him sharply. There was a crashing and breaking of the brittle, spongy growths. Twin tapering antennæ appeared, and then a monster beetle lurched into the open space, its horrible, gaping jaws stretched wide.

It was all of eight feet long, and its body was held up from the ground by six crooked, saw-toothed limbs. Its huge multiple eyes stared with machinelike preoccupation at the world.

It advanced deliberately, with a clanking and clashing as of a hideous machine. Burl fled on the instant, running as madly away from the beetle as he had a moment before been running toward it.

A little depression in the earth was before him. He did not swerve, but made to leap it. As he shot over it, however, the glint of pink skin caught his eye, and there was impressed upon his brain with photographic completeness the picture of Saya, lying limp and helpless, sinking slowly into the ground, with tiny rills of earth falling down the sides of the excavation upon her. It seemed to Burl's eye that she quivered slightly as he saw.

There was a terrific struggle within Burl. Behind him the colossal meat-eating beetle. Beneath him Saya, whom he loved. There was certain death lurching toward him on evilly glittering legs, and there was life for his race and tribe lying in the shallow pit.

He turned, aware with a sudden reckless glow that he was throwing away his life, aware that he was deliberately giving himself over to death, and stood on the side of the little pit nearest the great beetle, his puny spear held defiantly at the ready. In his left hand he held just such a leg as those which bore the living creature toward him. He had torn it from the body of just such a monster but a few hours ago, a monster in whose death he had had a share. With a yell of insane defiance, he flung the fiercely toothed limb at his advancing opponent.

The sharp teeth cut into the base of one of the beetle's antennæ, and it ducked clumsily, then seized the missile in its fierce jaws and crushed it in frenzy of rage. There was meat within it, sweet and juicy meat that pleased the beetle's palate.

It forgot the man, standing there, waiting for death. It crunched the missile that had attacked it, eating the palatable contents of the horny armor, confusing the blow with the object that had delivered it, and evidently satisfied that an enemy had been conquered and was being devoured. A moment later it turned and lumbered off to investigate another mushroom thicket.

And Burl turned quickly and dragged Saya's limp form from the grave that had been prepared for it by the busy insect scavengers. Earth fell from her shoulders, from her hair, and from the mass of yellow fur about her middle, and three little beetles with black and red markings scurried in terrified haste for cover, while Burl bore Saya to a resting-place of soft mold.

Burl was an ignorant savage, and to him Saya's deathlike unconsciousness was like death itself, but dumb misery smote him, and he laid her down gently, while tears came to his eyes and he called her name again and again in an agony of grief.

For an hour he sat there beside her, a man so lately pleased with himself above all creatures for having slain one huge beetle and put another to flight, as he would have looked upon it, now a broken-hearted, little pink-skinned man, weeping like a child, hunched up and bowed over with sorrow.

MURRAY LEINSTER

Then Saya slowly opened her eyes and stirred weakly.

THE FOREST OF DEATH

They were oblivious to everything but each other, Saya resting in still half-incredulous happiness against Burl's shoulder while he told her in little, jerky sentences of his pursuit of the colossal flying beetle, of his search for the tribe, and then his discovery of her apparently lifeless body.

When he spoke of the monster that had lurched from the mushroom thicket, and of the desperation with which he had faced it, Saya pressed close and looked at him with wondering and wonderful eyes. She could understand his willingness to die, believing her dead. A little while before she had felt the same indifference to life.

A timid, frightened whisper roused them from their absorption, and they looked up. One of the tribesmen stood upon one foot some distance away, staring at them, almost convinced that he looked upon the living dead. A sudden movement on the part of either of them would have sent him in a panic back into the mushroom forest. Two or three blond heads bobbed and vanished among the tangled stalks. Wide and astonished eyes gazed at the two they had believed the prey of malignant creatures.

The tribe had come slowly back to the mushroom they had been eating, leaderless, and convinced that Saya had fallen a victim to the deadly dust. Instead, they found her sitting by the side of their chief, apparently restored to them in some miraculous fashion.

Burl spoke, and the pink-skinned people came timorously from their hiding-places. They approached warily and formed a half-circle before the seated pair. Burl spoke again, and presently one of the bravest dared approach and touch him. Instantly a babble of the crude and labial language spoken by the tribe broke out. Awed questions and exclamations of thankfulness, then curious interrogations filled the air.

Burl, for once, showed some common sense. Instead of telling them in his usual vainglorious fashion of the adventures he had undergone, he merely cast down the two long and tapering antennæ from the

41

flying beetle that he had torn from its dead body. They looked at them, and recognized their origin. Amazement and admiration showed upon their faces. Then Burl rose and abruptly ordered two of the men to make a chair of their hands for Saya. She was weak from the effects of the blow she had received. The two men humbly advanced and did as they were bid.

Then the march was taken up again, more slowly than before, because of Saya as a burden, but none the less steadily. Burl led his people across the country, marching in advance and with every nerve alert for signs of danger, but with more confidence and less timidity than he had ever displayed before.

All that noontime and that afternoon they filed steadily along, the tribesfolk keeping in a compact group close behind Burl. The man who had thrown away his spear had recovered it on an order from Burl, and the little party fairly bristled with weapons, though Burl knew well that they were liable to be cast away as impediments if flight should be necessary.

He was determined that his people should learn to fight the great creatures about them, instead of depending upon their legs for escape. He had led them in an attack upon great slugs, but they were defenseless creatures, incapable of more dangerous maneuvers than spasmodic jerkings of their great bodies.

The next time danger should threaten them, and especially if it came while their new awe of him held good, he was resolved to force them to join him in fighting it.

He had not long to wait for an opportunity to strengthen the spirit of his followers by a successful battle. The clouds toward the west were taking on a dull-red hue, which was the nearest to a sunset that was ever seen in the world of Burl's experience, when a bumble bee droned heavily over their heads, making for its hive.

The little group of people on the ground looked up and saw a scanty load of pollen packed in the stiff bristles of the insect's hind legs. The bees of the world had a hard time securing food upon the nearly flowerless planet, but this one had evidently made a find. Its crop was nearly filled with hard-gathered, viscous honey destined for the hival store.

It sped onward, heavily, its almost transparent wings mere blurs in the air from the rapidity of their vibration. Burl saw its many-faceted eyes staring before it in worried preoccupation as it soared in laborious speed over his head, some fifty feet up.

He dropped his glance, and then his eyes lighted with excitement. A slender-bodied wasp was shooting upward from an ambush it had found in a thicket of toadstools. It darted swiftly and gracefully upon the bee, which swerved and tried to flee. The droning buzz of the bee's wings rose to a higher note as it strove to increase its speed. The more delicately formed wasp headed the clumsier insect back.

The bee turned again and fled in terror. Each of the insects was slightly more than four feet in length, but the bee was much the heavier, and it could not attain the speed of which the wasp was capable.

The graceful form of the hunting insect rapidly overhauled its fleeing prey, and the wasp dashed in and closed with the bee at a point almost over the heads of the tribesmen. In a clawing, biting tangle of thrashing, transparent wings and black bodies, the two creatures tumbled to the earth. They fell perhaps thirty yards from where Burl stood watching.

Over and over the two insects rolled, now one uppermost, and then the other. The bee was struggling desperately to insert her sting in the more supple body of her adversary. She writhed and twisted, fighting with jaw and mandible, wing and claw.

The wasp was uppermost, and the bee lay on her back, fighting in panic-stricken desperation. The wasp saw an opening, her jaws darted in, and there was an instant of confusion. Then suddenly the bee, dazed, was upright with the wasp upon her. A movement too quick for the eye to follow—and the bee collapsed. The wasp had bitten her in the neck where all the nerve-cords passed, and the bee was dead.

Burl waited a moment more, aflame with excitement. He knew, as did all the tribefolk, what might happen next. When he saw the second act of the tragedy well begun, Burl snapped quick and harsh orders to his spear-armed men, and they followed him in a wavering line, their weapons tightly clutched.

Knowing the habits of the insects as they were forced to know them, they knew that the venture was one of the least dangerous they could undertake with fighting creatures the size of the wasp, but the idea of attacking the great creatures whose sharp stings could annihilate any of them with a touch, the mere thought of taking the initiative was appalling. Had their awe of Burl been less complete they would not have dreamed of following him.

The second act of the tragedy had begun. The bee had been slain by the wasp, a carnivorous insect normally, but the wasp knew that sweet honey was concealed in the half-filled crop of the bee. Had the bee arrived safely at the hive, the sweet and sticky liquid would have been disgorged and added to the hival store. Now, though the bee's journey was ended and its flesh was to be crunched and devoured by the wasp, the honey was the first object of the pirate's solicitude. The dead insect was rolled over upon its back, and with eager haste the slayer began to exploit the body.

Burl and his men were creeping nearer, but with a gesture Burl bade them halt for a moment. The wasp's first move was to force the disgorgement of the honey from the bee's crop, and with feverish eagerness it pressed upon the limp body until the shining, sticky liquid appeared. Then the wasp began in ghoulish ecstasy to lick up the sweet stuff, utterly absorbed in the feast.

Many thousands of years before, the absorption of the then tiny insect had been noticed when engaged in a similar feat, and it was recorded in books moldered into dust long ages before Burl's birth that its rapture was so great that it had been known to fall a victim to a second bandit while engaged in the horrible banquet.

Burl had never read the books, but he had been told that the pirate would continue its feast even though seized by a greater enemy, unable to tear itself from the nectar gathered by the creature it had slain.

The tribesmen waited until the wasp had begun its orgy, licking up the toothsome stuff disgorged by its dead prey. It ate in gluttonous haste, blind to all sights, deaf to all sounds, able to think of nothing, conceive of nothing, but the delights of the liquid it was devouring.

At a signal the tribesmen darted forward. They wavered when near the slender-waisted gourmet, however, and Burl was the first to thrust his spear with all his strength into the thinly armored body.

Then the others took courage. A short, horny spear penetrated the very vitals of the wasp. A club fell with terrific impact upon the slender waist. There was a crackling, and the long, spidery limbs quivered and writhed, while the tribesmen fell back in fear, but without cause.

Burl struck again, and the wasp fell into two writhing halves, helpless for harm. The pink-skinned men danced in triumph, and the women and children ventured near, delighted.

Only Burl noticed that even as the wasp was dying, sundered and pierced with spears, its slender tongue licked out in one last, ecstatic taste of the nectar that had been its undoing.

Burdened with the pollen-covered legs of the giant bee, and filled with the meat from choice portions of the wasp's muscular limbs, the tribe resumed its journey. This time Burl had men behind him, still timid, still prone to flee at the slightest alarm, but infinitely more dependable than they had been before.

They had attacked and slain a wasp whose sting would have killed any of them. They had done battle under the leadership of Burl, whose spear had struck the first blow. Henceforth they were sharers, in a mild way, of his transcendent glory, and henceforth they were more like followers of a mighty chief and less like spineless worshipers of a demigod whose feats they were too timid to emulate.

That night they hid among a group of giant puff-balls, feasting on the loads of meat they had carried thus far with them. Burl watched them now without jealousy of their good spirits. He and Saya sat a little apart, happy to be near each other, speaking in low tones. After a time darkness fell, and the tribefolk became shapeless bodies speaking in voices that grew drowsy and were silent. The black forms of the toadstool heads and huge puff-balls were but darker against a dark sky.

The nightly rain began to fall, drop by drop, drop by drop, upon the damp and humid earth. Only Burl remained awake for a little while, and his last waking thought was of pride, disinterested pride. He had the first reward of the ruler, gratification in the greatness of his people.

THE RED DUST

The red mushrooms had continued to show their glistening heads, though Burl thought they were less numerous than in the territory from which the tribe had fled. All along the route, now to the right, now to the left, they had burst and sent their masses of deadly dust into the air.

Many times the tribefolk had been forced to make a detour to avoid a slowly spreading cloud of death-dealing spores. Once or twice their escapes had been narrow indeed, but so far there had been no deaths.

Burl had observed that the mushrooms normally burst only in the daytime, and for a while had thought of causing his followers to do their journeying in the night. Only the obvious disadvantages of such a course—the difficulty of discovering food, and the prowling spiders that roamed in the darkness—had prevented him. The idea still stayed with him, however, and two days after the fight with the hunting wasp he put it in practise.

The tribe came to the top of a small rise in the ground. For an hour they had been marching and counter-marching to avoid the suddenly appearing clouds of dust. Once they had been nearly hemmed in, and only by mad sprinting did they escape when three of the dull-red clouds seemed to flow together, closing three sides of a circle.

They came to the little hillock and halted. Before them stretched a plain all of four miles wide, colored a brownish brick-red by masses of mushrooms. They had seen mushroom forests before, and knew of the dangers they presented, but there was none so deadly as the plain before them. To right and left it stretched as far as the eye could see, but far away on its farther edge Burl caught a glimpse of flowing water.

Over the plain itself a dull-red haze seemed to float. It was nothing more or less than a cloud of the deadly spores, dispersed and indefinite, constantly replenished by the freshly bursting red mushrooms.

While the people stood and watched a dozen thick columns of dust rose into the air from scattered points here and there upon the plain, settling slowly again, but leaving behind them enough of their finely divided substance to keep the thin red haze over the whole plain in its original, deadly state.

MURRAY LEINSTER

Burl had seen single red mushrooms before, and even small thickets of two and three, but here was a plain of millions, literally millions upon millions of the malignant growths. Here was one fungoid forest through whose aisles no monster beetles stalked, and above whose shadowed depths no brightly colored butterflies fluttered in joyous abandon. There were no loud-voiced crickets singing in its hiding-places, nor bodies of eagerly foraging ants searching inquisitively for bits of food. It was a forest of death, still and silent, quiet and motionless save for the sullen columns of red dust that ever and again shot upward from the torn and ragged envelope of the bursting mushroom.

Burl and his people watched in wonderment and dismay, but presently a high resolve came to Burl. The mushrooms never burst at night, and the deadly dust from a subsided cloud was not deadly in the morning. As a matter of fact the rain that fell every night made it no more than a sodden, thin film of reddish mud by daybreak, mud which dried and caked.

Burl did not know what occurred, but knew the result. At night or in early morning, the danger from the red mushrooms was slight. Therefore he would lead his people through the very jaws of death that night. He would lead them through the deadly aisles of this, the forest of malignant growths, the place of lurking annihilation.

It was an act of desperation, and the resolution to carry it through left Burl in a state of mind that kept him from observing one thing that would have ended all the struggles of his tribe at once. Perhaps a quarter-mile from the edge of the red forest three or four giant cabbages grew, thrusting their colossal leaves upward toward the sky.

And on the cabbages a dozen lazy slugs fed leisurely, ignoring completely the red haze that was never far from them and sometimes covered them. Burl saw them, but the oddity of their immunity from the effects of the red dust did not strike him. He was fighting to keep his resolution intact. If he had only realized the significance of what he saw, however—

The slugs were covered with a thick soft fur. The tribespeople wore garments of that same material. The fur protected the slugs, and could have made the tribe immune to the deadly red dust if they had

47

only known. The slugs breathed through a row of tiny holes upon their backs, as the mature insects breathed through holes upon the bottom of their abdomens, and the soft fur formed a mat of felt which arrested the fine particles of deadly dust, while allowing the pure air to pass through. It formed, in effect, a natural gas-mask which the tribesmen should have adopted, but which they did not discover or invent.

The remainder of that day they waited in a curious mixture of resolve and fear. The tribe was rapidly reaching a point where it would follow Burl over a thousand-foot cliff, and it needed some such blind confidence to make them prepare to go through the forest of the million deadly mushrooms.

The waiting was a strain, but the actual journey was a nightmare. Burl knew that the toadstools did not burst of themselves during the night, but he knew that the beetle on which he had taken his involuntary ride had crashed against one in the darkness, and that the fatal dust had poured out. He warned his people to be cautious, and led them down the slope of the hill through the blackness.

For hours they stumbled on in utter darkness, with the pungent, acrid odor of the red growths constantly in their nostrils. They put out their hands and touched the flabby, damp stalks of the monstrous things. They stumbled and staggered against the leathery skins of the malignant fungoids.

Death was all about them. At no time during all the dark hours of the night was there a moment when they could not reach out their hands and touch a fungus growth that might burst at their touch and fill the air with poisonous dust, so that all of them would die in gasping, choking agony.

And worst of all, before half an hour was past they had lost all sense of direction, so that they stumbled on blindly through the utter blackness, not knowing whether they were headed toward the river that might be their salvation or were wandering hopelessly deeper and deeper into the silent depths of the forest of strangled things.

When day came again and the mushrooms sent their columns of fatal dust into the air would they gasp and fight for breath in the red haze that would float like a tenuous cloud above the forest? Would they breathe in flames of firelike torment and die slowly, or would the red dust be merciful and slay them quickly?

They felt their way like blind folk, devoid of hope and curiously unafraid. Only their hearts were like heavy, cold weights in their breasts, and they shouldered aside the swollen sacs of the red mushrooms with a singular apathy as they followed Burl slowly through the midst of death.

Many times in their journeying they knew that dead creatures were near by—moths, perhaps, that had blundered into a distended growth which had burst upon the impact and killed the thing that had touched it.

No busy insect scavengers ventured into this plain of silence to salvage the bodies, however. The red haze preserved the sanctuary of malignance inviolate. During the day no creature might hope to approach its red aisles and dust-carpeted clearings, and at night the slow-dropping rain fell only upon the rounded heads of the mushrooms.

In all the space of the forest, only the little band of hopeless people, plodding on behind Burl in the velvet blackness, callously rubbed shoulders with death in the form of the red and glistening mushrooms. Over all the dank expanse of the forest, the only sound was the dripping of the slow and sodden rainfall that began at nightfall and lasted until day came again.

The sky began to grow faintly gray as the sun rose behind the banks of overhanging clouds. Burl stopped short and uttered what was no more than a groan. He was in a little circular clearing, and the twisted, monstrous forms of the deadly mushrooms were all about. There was not yet enough light for colors to appear, and the hideous, almost obscene shapes of the loathsome growths on every side showed only as mocking, leering silhouettes as of malicious demons rejoicing at the coming doom of the gray-faced, huddled tribefolk.

Burl stood still, drooping in discouragement upon his spear, the feathery moth's antennæ bound upon his forehead shadowed darkly against the graying sky. Soon the mushrooms would begin to burst—

Then, suddenly, he lifted his head, encouragement and delight upon his features. He had heard the ripple of running water. His followers looked at him with dawning hope. Without a word, Burl began to run, and they followed him more slowly. His voice came back to them in a shout of delight.

Then they, too, broke into a jog-trot. In a moment they had emerged from the thick tangle of brownish-red stalks and were upon the banks of a wide and swiftly running river, the same river whose gleam Burl had caught the day before from the farther side of the mushroom forest.

Once before Burl had floated down a river upon a mushroom raft. Then his journey had been involuntary and unlooked for. He had been carried far from his tribe and far from Saya, and his heart had been filled with desolation.

Now he viewed the swiftly running current with eager delight. He cast his eyes up and down the bank. Here and there the river-bank rose in a low bluff, and thick shelf-growths stretched out above the water.

Burl was busy in an instant, stabbing the hard growths with his spear and striving to wrench them free. The tribesmen stared at him, uncomprehending, but at an order from him they did likewise.

Soon a dozen thick masses of firm, light fungus lay upon the shore where it shelved gently into the water. Burl began to explain what they were to do, but one or two of the men dared remonstrate, saying humbly that they were afraid to part from him. If they might embark upon the same thing with him, they would be safe, but otherwise they were afraid.

Burl cast an apprehensive glance at the sky. Day was coming rapidly on. Soon the red mushrooms would begin to shoot their columns of deadly dust into the air. This was no time to pause and deliberate. Then Saya spoke softly.

Burl listened, and made a mighty sacrifice. He took his gorgeous velvet cloak from his shoulders—it was made from the wing of a great moth—and tore it into a dozen long, irregular pieces, tearing it along the lines of the sinews that reinforced it. He planted his spear upright in the largest piece of shelf-fungus and caused his followers to do likewise, then fastened the strips of sinew and velvet to his spear-shaft, and ordered them to do the same to the other spears.

MURRAY LEINSTER

In a matter of minutes the dozen tiny rafts were bobbing on the water, clustered about the larger, central bit. Then, one by one, the tribefolk took their places, and Burl shoved off.

The agglomeration of cranky, unseaworthy bits of shelf-fungus moved slowly out from the shore until the current caught it. Burl and Saya sat upon the central bit, with the other trustful but somewhat frightened pink-skinned people all about them. And, as they began to move between the mushroom-lined banks of the river and the mist of the night began to lift from its surface, far in the interior of the forest of the red fungoids a column of sullen red leaped into the air. The first of the malignant growths had cast its cargo of poisonous dust into the still-humid atmosphere.

The conelike column spread out and grew thin, but even after it had sunk into the earth, a reddish taint remained in the air about the place where it had been. The deadly red haze that hung all through the day over the red forest was in process of formation.

But by that time the unstable fungus rafts were far down the river, bobbing and twirling in the current, with the wide-eyed people upon them gazing in wonderment at the shores as they glided by. The red mushrooms grew less numerous upon the banks. Other growths took their places. Molds and rusts covered the ground as grass had done in ages past. Mushrooms showed their creamy, rounded heads. Malformed things with swollen trunks and branches in strange mockery of the trees they had superseded made their appearance, and once the tribesmen saw the dark bulk of a hunting spider outlined for a moment upon the bank.

All the long day they rode upon the current, while the insect life that had been absent in the neighborhood of the forest of death made its appearance again. Bees once more droned overhead, and wasps and dragon-flies. Four-inch mosquitoes made their appearance, to be fought off by the tribefolk with lusty blows, and glittering beetles and shining flies, whose bodies glittered with a metallic luster, buzzed and flew above the water.

Huge butterflies once more were seen, dancing above the steaming, festering earth in an apparent ecstasy from the mere fact of existence, and all the thousand and one forms of insect life that flew and

51

crawled, and swam and dived, showed themselves to the tribesmen on the raft.

Water-beetles came lazily to the surface, to snap with sudden energy at mosquitoes busily laying their eggs in the nearly stagnant water by the river-banks. Burl pointed out to Saya, with some excitement, their silver breast-plates that shone as they darted under the water again. And the shell-covered boats of a thousand caddis-worms floated in the eddies and back-waters of the stream. Water-boatmen and whirligigs—almost alone among insects in not having shared in the general increase of size—danced upon the oily waves.

The day wore on as the shores flowed by. The tribefolk ate of their burdens of mushroom and meat, and drank from the fresh water of the river. Then, when afternoon came, the character of the country about the stream changed. The banks fell away, and the current slackened. The shores became indefinite, and the river merged itself into a swamp, a vast swamp from which a continual muttering came which the tribesmen heard for a long time before they saw the swamp itself.

The water seemed to turn dark, as black mud took the place of the clay that had formed its bed, and slowly, here and there, then more frequently, floating green things that were stationary, and did not move with the current, appeared. They were the leaves of water-lilies, that had remained with the giant cabbages and a very few other plants in the midst of a fungoid world. The green leaves were twelve feet across, and any one of them would have floated the whole of Burl's tribe.

Presently they grew numerous so that the channel was made narrow, and the mushroom rafts passed between rows of the great leaves, with here and there a colossal, waxen blossom in which three men might have hidden and which exhaled an almost over-powering fragrance into the air.

And the muttering that had been heard far away grew in volume to an intermittent, incredibly deep bass roar. It seemed to come from the banks on either side, and actually was the discordant croaking of the giant frogs, grown to eight feet in length, which lived and loved in the huge swamp, above which golden butterflies danced in ecstasy, and which the transcendently beautiful blossoms of the water-lilies filled with fragrance.

The swamp was a place of riotous life. The green bodies of the colossal frogs—perched upon the banks in strange immobility and only opening their huge mouths to emit their thunderous croakings—the green bodies of the frogs blended queerly with the vivid color of the water-lily leaves. Dragon-flies fluttered in their swift and angular flight above the black and reeking mud. Green-bottles and blue-bottles and a hundred other species of flies buzzed busily in the misty air, now and then falling prey to the licking tongues of the frogs.

Bees droned overhead in flight less preoccupied and worried than elsewhere flitting from blossom to blossom of the tremendous water-lilies, loading their crops with honey and the bristles of their legs with yellow pollen.

Everywhere over the mushroom-covered world the air was never quite free from mist, and the steaming exhalations of the pools, but here in the swamps the atmosphere was so heavily laden with moisture that the bodies of the tribefolk were covered with glistening droplets, while the wide, flat water-lily leaves glittered like platters of jewels from the "steam" that had condensed upon their upper surfaces.

The air was full of shining bodies and iridescent wings. Myriads of tiny midges—no more than three or four inches across their wings—danced above the slow-flowing water. And butterflies of every imaginable shade and color, from the most delicate lavender to the most vivid carmine, danced and fluttered, alighting upon the white water-lilies to sip daintily of their nectar, skimming the surface of the water, enamored of their brightly tinted reflections.

And the pink-skinned tribesfolk, floating through this fairyland on their mushroom rafts, gazed with wide eyes at the beauty about them, and drew in great breaths of the intoxicating fragrance of the great white flowers that floated like elfin boats upon the dark water.

THE RED DUST

OUT OF BONDAGE

The mist was heavy and thick, and through it the flying creatures darted upon their innumerable businesses, visible for an instant in all their colorful beauty, then melting slowly into indefiniteness as they sped away. The tribefolk on the clustered rafts watched them as they darted overhead, and for hours the little squadron of fungoid vessels floated slowly through the central channel of the marsh.

The river had split into innumerable currents which meandered purposelessly through the glistening black mud of the swamp, but after a long time they seemed to reassemble, and Burl could see what had caused the vast morass.

Hills appeared on either side of the stream, which grew higher and steeper, as if the foothills of a mountain chain. Then Burl turned and peered before him.

Rising straight from the low hills, a wall of high mountains rose toward the sky, and the low-hanging clouds met their rugged flanks but half-way toward the peaks. To right and left the mountains melted into the tenuous haze, but ahead they were firm and stalwart, rising and losing their heights in the cloud-banks.

They formed a rampart which might have guarded the edge of the world, and the river flowed more and more rapidly in a deeper and narrower current toward a cleft between two rugged giants that promised to swallow the water and all that might swim in its depths or float upon its surface.

Tall, steep hills rose from either side of the swift current, their sides covered with flaking molds of an exotic shade of rose-pink, mingled here and there with lavender and purple. Rocks, not hidden beneath a coating of fungus, protruded their angular heads from the hillsides. The river valley became a gorge, and then little more than a cañon, with beetling sides that frowned down upon the swift current running beneath them.

The small flotilla passed beneath an overhanging cliff, and then shot out to where the cliffsides drew apart and formed a deep amphitheater, whose top was hidden in the clouds.

And across this open space, on cables all of five hundred feet long, a banded spider had flung its web. It was a monster of its tribe. Its

54

belly was swollen to a diameter of no less than two yards, and its outstretched legs would have touched eight points of a ten-yard circle.

It was hanging motionless in the center of the colossal snare as the little group of tribefolk passed underneath, and they saw the broad bands of yellow and black and silver upon its abdomen. They shivered as their little crafts were swept below.

Then they came to a little valley, where yellow sand bordered the river and there was a level space of a hundred yards on either side before the steep sides of the mountains began their rise. Here the cluster of mushroom rafts were caught in a little eddy and drawn out of the swiftly flowing current. Soon there was a soft and yielding jar. The rafts had grounded.

Led by Burl, the tribesmen waded ashore, wonderment and excitement in their hearts. Burl searched all about with his eyes. Toadstools and mushrooms, rusts and molds, even giant puff-balls grew in the little valley, but of the deadly red mushrooms he saw none.

A single bee was buzzing slowly over the tangled thickets of fungoids, and the loud voice of a cricket came in a deafening burst of sound, reechoed from the hillsides, but save for the far-flung web of the banded spider a mile or more away, there was no sign of the deadly creatures that preyed upon men.

Burl began to climb the hillside with his tribefolk after him. For an hour they toiled upward, through confused masses of fungus of almost every species. Twice they stopped to seize upon edible fungi and break them into masses they could carry, and once they paused and made a wide detour around a thicket from which there came a stealthy rustling.

Burl believed that the rustling was merely the sound of a moth or butterfly emerging from its chrysalis, but was unwilling to take any chances. He and his people circled the mushroom thicket and mounted higher.

And at last, perhaps six or seven hundred feet above the level of the river, they came upon a little plateau, going back into a small pocket in the mountainside. Here they found many of the edible fungoids, and no less than a dozen of the giant cabbages, on whose broad leaves many furry grubs were feeding steadily in placid contentment with themselves and all the world.

A small stream bubbled up from a tiny basin and ran swiftly across the plateau, and there were dense thickets of toadstools in which the tribesmen might find secure hiding-places. The tribe would make itself a new home here.

That night they hid among inextricably tangled masses of mushrooms, and saw with amazement the multitude of creatures that ventured forth in the darkness. All the valley and the plateau were illumined by the shining beacons of huge but graceful fireflies, who darted here and there in delight and—apparently—in security.

Upon the earth below, also, many tiny lights glowed. The larvæ of the fireflies crawled slowly but happily over the fungus-covered mountainside, and great glow-worms clambered upon the shining tops of the toadstools and rested there, twin broad bands of bluish fire burning brightly within their translucent bodies.

They were the females of the firefly race, which never attain to legs and wings, but crawl always upon the earth, merely enlarged creatures in the forms of their own larvæ. Moths soared overhead with mighty, throbbing wing-beats, and all the world seemed a paradise through which no evil creatures roamed in search of prey.

And a strange thing came to pass. Soon after darkness fell upon the earth and the steady drip-drop of the rain began, a musical tinkling sound was heard which grew in volume, and became a deep-toned roar, which reechoed and reverberated from the opposite hillsides until it was like melodious and long-continued thunder. For a long time the people were puzzled and a little afraid, but Burl took courage and investigated.

He emerged from the concealing thicket and peered cautiously about, seeing nothing. Then he dared move in the direction of the sound, and the gleam from a dozen fireflies showed him a sheet of water pouring over a vertical cliff to the river far below.

The rainfall, gentle as it was, when gathered from all the broad expanse of the mountainside, made a river of its own, which had scoured out a bed, and poured down each night to plunge in a smother of spray and foam through six hundred feet of empty space to the swiftly flowing river in the center of the valley. It was this sound that had puzzled the tribefolk, and this sound that lulled them to sleep when Burl at last came back to allay their fears.

The next day they explored their new territory with a boldness of which they would not have been capable a month before. They found a single great trap-door in the earth, sure sign of the burrow of a monster spider, and Burl resolved that before many days the spider would be dealt with. He told his tribesmen so, and they nodded their heads solemnly instead of shrinking back in terror as they would have done not long since.

The tribe was rapidly becoming a group of men, capable of taking the aggressive. They needed Burl's rash leadership, and for many generations they would need bold leaders, but they were infinitely superior to the timid, rabbit-like creatures they had been. They bore spears, and they had used them. They had seen danger, and had blindly followed Burl through the forest of strangled things instead of fleeing weakly from the peril.

They wore soft, yellow fur about their middles, taken from the bodies of giant slugs they had slain. They had eaten much meat, and preferred its succulent taste to the insipid savor of the mushrooms that had once been their steady diet. They knew the exhilaration of brave adventure—though they had been forced into adventure by Burl—and they were far more worthy descendants of their ancestors than those ancestors had known for many thousand years.

The exploration of their new domain yielded many wonders and a few advantages. The tribefolk found that the nearest ant-city was miles away, and that the small insects would trouble them but rarely. (The nightly rush of water down the sloping sides of the mountain made it undesirable for the site of an ant colony.)

And best of all, back in the little pocket in the mountainside, they found old and disused cells of hunting wasps. The walls of the pocket were made of soft sandstone with alternate layers of clay, and the wasps had found digging easy.

There were a dozen or more burrows, the shaft of each some four feet in diameter and going back into the cliff for nearly thirty feet, where they branched out into a number of cells. Each of the cells had once held a grub which had grown fat and large upon its hoard of paralyzed crickets, and then had broken away to the outer world to emerge as a full-grown wasp.

Now, however, the laboriously tunneled caverns would furnish a hiding-place for the tribe of men, a far more secure hiding-place than the center of the mushroom thickets. And, furthermore, a hiding-place which, because more permanent, would gradually become a possession for which the men would fight.

It is a curious thing that the advancement of a people from a state of savagery and continual warfare to civilization and continual peace is not made by the elimination of the causes of strife, but by the addition of new objects and ideals, in defense of which that same people will offer battle.

A single chrysalis was found securely anchored to the underside of a rock-shelf, and Burl detached it with great labor and carried it into one of the burrows, though the task was one that was almost beyond his strength. He desired the butterfly that would emerge for his own use.

He preempted, too, a solitary burrow a little distant from the others, and made preparations for an event that was destined to make his plans wiser and more far-reaching than before.

His followers were equally busy with their various burrows, gathering stores of soft growth for their couches, and later—at Burl's suggestion—even carrying within the dark caverns the radiant heads of the luminous mushrooms to furnish illumination. The light would be dim, and after the mushroom had partly dried it would cease, but for a people utterly ignorant of fire it was far from a bad plan.

Burl was very happy for that time. His people looked upon him as a savior, and obeyed his least order without question. He was growing to repose some measure of trust in them, too, as men who began to have some glimmerings of the new-found courage that had come to him, and which he had striven hard to implant in their breasts.

The tribe had been a formless gathering of people. There were six or seven men and as many women, and naturally families had come into being—sometimes after fierce and absurd fights among the men—but the families were not the sharply distinct agreements they would have been in a tribe of higher development.

The marriage was but an agreement, terminable at any time, and the men had but little of the feeling of parenthood, though the women had all the fierce maternal instinct of the insects about them.

These burrows in which the tribefolk were making their homes would put an end to the casual nature of the marriage bonds. They were homes in the making—damp and humid burrows without fire or heat, but homes, nevertheless. The family may come before the home, in the development of mankind, but it invariably exists when the home has been made.

The tribe had been upon the plateau for nearly a week when Burl found that stirrings and strugglings were going on within the huge cocoon he had laid close beside the burrow he had chosen for his own. He cast aside all other work, and waited patiently for the thing he knew was about to happen. He squatted on his haunches beside the huge, oblong cylinder, his spear in his hand, waiting patiently. From time to time he nibbled at a bit of edible mushroom.

Burl had acquired many new traits, among which a little foresight was most prominent, but he had never conquered the habit of feeling hungry at any and every time that food was near at hand. He had to wait. He had food. Therefore, he ate.

The sound of scrapings came from the closed cocoon, caked upon its outer side with dirt and mold. The scraping and scratching continued, and presently a tiny hole showed, which rapidly enlarged. Tiny jaws and a dry, glazed skin became visible, the skin looking as if it had been varnished with many coats of brown shellac. Then a malformed head forced its way through and stopped.

All motion ceased for a matter of perhaps half an hour, and then the strange, blind head seemed to become distended, to be swelling. A crack appeared along its upper part, which lengthened and grew wide. And then a second head appeared from within the first.

This head was soft and downy, and a slender proboscis was coiled beneath its lower edge like the trunk of one of the elephants that had been extinct for many thousand years. Soft scales and fine hairs alternated to cover it, and two immense, many-faceted eyes gazed mildly at the world on which it was looking for the first time. The color of the whole was purest milky-white.

Slowly and painfully, assisting itself by slender, colorless legs that seemed strangely feeble and trembling, a butterfly crawled from the cocoon. Its wings were folded and lifeless, without substance or color, but the body was a perfect white. The butterfly moved a little distance from its cocoon and slowly unfurled its wings. With the action, life seemed to be pumped into them from some hidden spring in the insect's body. The slender antennæ spread out and wavered gently in the warm air. The wings were becoming broad expanses of snowy velvet.

A trace of eagerness seemed to come into the butterfly's actions. Somewhere there in the valley sweet food and joyous companions awaited it. Fluttering above the fungoids of the hillsides, surely there was a mate with whom the joys of love were to be shared, surely upon those gigantic patches of green, half hidden in the haze, there would be laid tiny golden eggs that in time would hatch into small, fat grubs.

Strength came to the butterfly's limbs. Its wings were spread and closed with a new assurance. It spread them once more, and raised them to make the first flight of this new existence in a marvelous world, full of delights and adventures—Burl struck home with his spear.

The delicate limbs struggled in agony, the wings fluttered helplessly, and in a little while the butterfly lay still upon the fungus-carpeted earth, and Burl leaned over to strip away the great wings of snow-white velvet, to sever the long and slender antennæ, and then to call his tribesmen and bid them share in the food he had for them.

And there was a feast that afternoon. The tribesmen sat about the white carcass, cracking open the delicate limbs for the meat within them, and Burl made sure that Saya secured the choicest bits. The tribesmen were happy. Then one of the children of the tribe stretched a hand aloft and pointed up the mountainside.

Coming slowly down the slanting earth was a long, narrow file of living animals. For a time the file seemed to be but one creature, but Burl's keen eyes soon saw that there were many. They were caterpillars, each one perhaps ten feet long, each with a tiny black head armed with sharp jaws, and with dull-red fur upon their backs. The rear of the procession was lost in the mist of the low-hanging cloud-banks that covered the mountainside some two thousand feet above the plateau, but the foremost was no more than three hundred yards away.

Slowly and solemnly the procession came on, the black head of the second touching the rear of the first, and the head of the third touching the rear of the second. In faultless alignment, without intervals, they moved steadily down the slanting side of the mountain.

Save the first, they seemed absorbed in maintaining their perfect formation, but the leader constantly rose upon his hinder half and waved the fore part of his body in the air, first to the right and then to the left, as if searching out the path he would follow.

The tribefolk watched in amazement mingled with terror. Only Burl was calm. He had never seen a slug that meant danger to man, and he reasoned that these were at any rate moving slowly so that they could be distanced by the fleeter-footed human beings, but he also meant to be cautious.

The slow march kept on. The rear of the procession of caterpillars emerged from the cloud-bank, and Burl saw that a shining white line was left behind them. No less than eighty great caterpillars clad in white and dingy red were solemnly moving down the mountainside, leaving a path of shining silk behind them. Head to tail, in single file, they had no eyes or ears for anything but their procession.

The leader reached the plateau, and turned. He came to the cluster of giant cabbages, and ignored them. He came to a thicket of mushrooms, and passed through it, followed by his devoted band. Then he came to an open space where the earth was soft and sandy, where sandstone had weathered and made a great heap of easily moved earth.

The leading caterpillar halted, and began to burrow experimentally in the ground. The result pleased him, and some signal seemed to pass along the eight-hundred-foot line of creatures. The leader began to dig with feet and jaws, working furiously to cover himself completely with the soft earth. Those immediately behind him abandoned their formation, and pressed forward in haste. Those still farther back moved more hurriedly.

All, when they reached the spot selected by the leader, abandoned any attempt to keep to their line, and hastened to find an unoccupied spot in the open space in which to bury themselves.

For perhaps half an hour the clearing was the scene of intense activity, incredible activity. Huge, ten-foot bodies burrowed desperately in the whitish earth, digging frantically to cover themselves.

After the half-hour, however, the last of the caterpillars had vanished. Only an occasional movement of the earth from the struggle of a buried creature to bury itself still deeper, and the freshly turned surface showed that beneath the clearing on the plateau eighty great slugs were preparing themselves for the sleep of metamorphosis. The piled-up earth and the broad, white band of silk, leading back up the hillside until it became lost in the clouds, alone remained to tell of the visitation.

The tribesmen had watched in amazement. They had never seen these creatures before, but they knew, of course, why they had entombed themselves. Had they known what the scientists of thirty thousand years before had written in weighty and dull books, they would have deduced from the appearance of the processionary caterpillars—or pine-caterpillars—that somewhere above the banks of clouds there were growing trees and sunlight, that a moon shone down, and stars twinkled from the blue vault of a cloudless sky.

But the tribesmen did not know. They only knew that there, beneath the soft earth, was a mighty store of food for them when they cared to dig for it, that their provisions for many months were secure, and that Burl, their leader, was a great and mighty man for having led them to this land of safety and plenty.

Burl read their emotions in their eyes, but better than their amazement and wonderment was a glance that had nothing whatever to do with his leadership of the tribe. And then Burl rose, and took the two snowy-white velvet cloaks from the wings of the white butterfly. One of them he flung about his own shoulders, and the other he flung about Saya. And then those two stood up before the wide-eyed tribesmen, and Burl spoke:

"This is my mate, and my food is her food, and her wrath is my wrath. My burrow is her burrow, and her sorrow, my sorrow.

"Men whom I have led to this land of plenty, hear me. As ye obey my words, see to it that the words of Saya are obeyed likewise, for my spear will loose the life from any man who angers her. Know that as I am great beyond all other men, so Saya is great beyond all other women, for I say it, and it is so."

And he drew Saya toward him, trembling slightly, and put his arm about her waist before all the tribe, and the tribesmen muttered in acquiescent whispers that what Burl said was true, as they had already known.

Then, while the pink-skinned men feasted on the meat Burl had provided for them, he and Saya went toward the burrow he had made ready. It was not like the other burrows, being set apart from them, and its entrance was bordered on either side by mushrooms as black as night. All about the entrance the black mushrooms clustered, a strange species that grew large and scattered its spores abroad and then of its own accord melted into an inky liquid that flowed away, sinking slowly into the ground.

In a little hollow below the opening of the burrow an inky pool had gathered, which reflected the gray clouds above and the shapes of the mushrooms that overhung its edges.

Burl and Saya made their way toward the burrow in silence, a picturesque couple against the black background of the sable mushrooms and the earth made dark by the inky liquid. Both of their figures were swathed in cloaks of unsmirched whiteness and wondrous softness, and bound to Burl's forehead were the feathery, lacelike antenna of a great moth, making flowing plumes of purest gold. His spear seemed cast from bronze, and he was a proud figure as he led Saya past the black pool and to the doorway of their home.

They sat there, watching, while the darkness came on and the moths and fireflies emerged to dance in the night, and listened when the rain began its slow, deliberate dripping from the heavy clouds above. Presently a gentle rumbling began—the accumulation of the rain from all the mountainside forming a torrent that would pour in a six-hundred-foot drop to the river far below.

The sound of the rushing water grew louder, and was echoed back from the cliffs on the other side of the valley. The fireflies danced like fairy lights in the chasm, and all the creatures of the night winged their way aloft to join in the ecstasy of life and love.

And then, when darkness was complete, and only the fitful gleams of the huge fireflies were reflected from the still surface of the black pool beneath their feet, Burl reached out his hand to Saya, sitting beside him in the darkness. She yielded shyly, and her soft, warm hand found his in the obscurity. And Burl bent over and kissed her on the lips.